I0556360

Twisted Beautiee 4
An Erotic Thriller

Twisted Beautiee 4
An Erotic Thriller

BY

TRACY WILSON

http://beautifulpublications.com

Published by
Beautiful Publications LLC
Stratford, CT 06614

This book is a work of fiction. Names, characters, places, and incidents are either products of the author's imagination or are used fictitiously. Any resemblance to actual events or locales or persons, living or dead, is entirely coincidental.

©Copyright 2019 Tracy Wilson

All rights reserved. No part of this publication may be reproduced or transmitted in any form or by any means, electronic or mechanical, including photocopy, recording, or any information storage and retrieval system, without permission in writing from the copyright owner, except by a reviewer who may quote brief passages in a review.

PRINT ISBN: 978-1-7331792-0-1
EBOOK ISBN: 978-1-7331792-9-4

Printed in the United States of America

Dedication

I dedicate this series to my alter ego, Beautiee.

Published by
Beautiful Publications LLC
Stratford, CT 06614

This book is a work of fiction. Names, characters, places, and incidents are either products of the author's imagination or are used fictitiously. Any resemblance to actual events or locales or persons, living or dead, is entirely coincidental.

©Copyright 2019 Tracy Wilson

All rights reserved. No part of this publication may be reproduced or transmitted in any form or by any means, electronic or mechanical, including photocopy, recording, or any information storage and retrieval system, without permission in writing from the copyright owner, except by a reviewer who may quote brief passages in a review.

PRINT ISBN: 978-1-7331792-0-1
EBOOK ISBN: 978-1-7331792-9-4

Printed in the United States of America

Dedication

I dedicate this series to my alter ego, Beautiee.

Chapter 1

"Beautiee!" Bazil whispered as he stuck his head out the door. I looked to the left then to the right... "Over here!" I turned around and saw him sticking his head out a door at the end of the hallway and I ran towards him. When I got to the door, Bazil snatched me inside, closed the door, and locked it...

"Dammit – where the hell is she?" Smalls asked as he looked for me in the attorney-client room... "Shit – I hope she's in the ladies room – I'ma start eating – I hope she comes back so she can eat..." he said as he started eating...

"Where are we?" I whispered...
"We're in Judge Duffey's old chambers..." he answered as he started kissing me on my neck...
"Bazil..." I moaned...
"Ssshhhh..." he said before he pulled my face to his and forced his tongue in my mouth. We continued kissing feverishly as Bazil unzipped my prison jumpsuit and slid it off my shoulders...
"Bazil..." I moaned, whispering as he pushed me against the wall and began sucking

my breasts, alternating between the left and the right... and I started to cry. Bazil turned me away from the wall, braced himself against the wall, and dropped his pants. His dick was a sight for sore eyes – and I wanted it bad – so I squatted down...

"Beautiee..." Bazil moaned as I took him in my mouth completely. I slid my hands up to his ass and grabbed it while Bazil simultaneously grabbed my head and fucked my mouth...

"Mmmmmm...." I moaned on his dick...

"Beautiee... it's been so long... fuck!" he moaned as he came in my mouth. I swallowed every last drop and continued sucking for a few moments...

"Judge Duffey – your wife is on line one – she asked me to – what the hell is that?" the Bailiff asked as he looked over Judge Duffey's shoulder and saw him watching us...

"What's it look like?" Judge Duffey answered, smiling mischievously...

"It looks like they're fucking in your chambers! I'ma go put a stop to this shit right now!"

"Leave it..." Judge Duffey ordered as he continued watching us...

"Leave it?"

"Yes..."

"Very well – I'll go tell you wife you're in the middle of something..."

"Yes... do that..." Judge Duffey said as the Bailiff closed the door. Judge Duffey put his hand under the desk, pulled his dick out, and began stroking it as he continued watching us...

"Beautiee... get up..." Bazil said as he pulled me up and into a kiss...

"I love you my Thirst Quencher..." I breathed..."

"I love you too – come with me..." he said as he took me by the hand and pulled me towards the bench in front of the judges' bench and pushed me down on my back. Bazil lifted me up, slid my prison jumpsuit off, spread my legs, and dove in...

"Oh Bazil!" I moaned...

"I know baby... I know..." he said as he continued licking... "But I need you to be quiet..."

"It's so good... I can't..." I whispered...

"Here... bite down on this..." he said as he took a handkerchief out his pocket and stuffed it into my mouth...

"MmmmMmmmMmmm!" I moaned as Bazil devoured my pussy with his mouth. He continued licking, slurping, and sucking as I rode his face and moaned and then he slid two fingers inside me... and I lost it... "Bazil... Fuck... I'm Cummmmiiinnngggg!" I whispered as I dug my fingers into the sides of his head...

"I swear... you couldn't be quiet if our life depended on it..." he laughed as he kissed his way up my body and lay between my legs..."

"Fuck me Bazil..." I whispered... "Please..."

"I intend to..." he growled as he thrust himself inside me. Bazil covered my mouth with his and thrust his tongue inside my mouth to keep me from crying out as he fucked me hard and fast. We didn't give a damn about being caught as the bench started banging on the floor with each thrust...

"Bang! Bang! Bang!"

"What the fuck on going on in there?" a second Bailiff asked...

"Construction," the court Bailiff laughed as he came towards the door...

"Did Judge Duffey order it? You know how he is when it comes to his chambers," the second Bailiff said.

"He's aware of it – don't worry about it..." the court Bailiff said.

"Okay – I'ma head back to my room – lunch is almost over..." the second Bailiff said.

"I'll head back too – I need to let Judge Duffey know it's just about 1 o'clock..." the court Bailiff said as he went towards Judge Duffey's current chambers...

"I love you Beautiee..." Bazil breathed...

"I love you too..." I said as I started to cry...

"Ssshhh... don't cry Beautiee..." he said as he kissed my tears..."

"I can't help it... I'm so happy..."

"Damn – I needed that..." Judge Duffey said as he finished wiping his dick off. He put his dick back in his pants just in time...

"Your honor – lunch is over..." the Bailiff said as he came inside... "You want me to go get the defendant?"

"Yes..." Judge Duffey answered... "But give her a minute to get dressed..." he laughed...

"Oh – so you saw that?" the Bailiff laughed...

"I sure did..." Judge Duffey said as he smiled mischievously...

"I heard it!" The Bailiff laughed...

"No shit!" Judge Duffey laughed...

"Bang! Bang! Bang!" the Bailiff laughed...

"Poor thing hasn't had any dick since she's been incarcerated – and from what I saw – she needed it – bad! Haaaaa...... Haaaaa....."

"You ain't right!" the Bailiff laughed...

"I love this job!" Judge Duffey laughed...

"Are you going to punish her?" the Bailiff asked...

"Naaa... but when this trial is over – I'm going to send them a little gift to show them my appreciation!" Judge Duffey laughed...

"Oh shit! You still have cameras in there?"

"Of course..."

"I'ma go get the defendant now..." the Bailiff laughed as he headed down the hall...

"Shit – it's just about 1 o'clock – Beautiee c'mon..." Smalls said out loud as he headed for the court room. When he got there he saw Troy and Keisha sitting in the back. "Yo – where's Bazil?"

"I'on know – we ain't seen him since we got back..." Keisha said.

"Oh God – I don't see Beautiee either – I got a bad feeling..."

"They somewhere fuckin'!" Troy laughed...

"I hope not – I gotta get to the table..." Smalls said as he went to the table and sat down...

"Beautiee – get up – somebody's coming!" Bazil breathed as he snatched me up and helped me put my jumpsuit back on...

"Open this door – now!" the Bailiff yelled from the other side of the door...

"I'm coming!" I answered as Bazil dipped into the private bathroom. Once I saw he was in the bathroom I unlocked the door and opened it...

"You had no business in here – you know that – right?" the Bailiff asked as he snatched me by the arm...

"Yes..." I answered...

"Let's go – Judge Duffey already told you he doesn't like to be kept waiting..." he said as he pulled me out the judge's chambers and down the hall to the court room. Once I got inside the court room and I was seated next to Smalls, Bazil came into the court room and sat in the back.

"Where the hell were you?" Smalls whispered...

"I was with Bazil..." I whispered as I smiled...

"All rise..."the Bailiff said. Everyone stood up. "Department One of the Superior Court is now in session. Judge Duffey presiding. Please be seated."

"Calling the case of the People of the State of Connecticut versus Beautiee Osgood. Are both sides ready?"

"Ready for the People, Your Honor..." Beverly said.

"Ready for the Defense, Your Honor..." Smalls said.

"Beverly – you may call your next witness..." Judge Duffey said...

"Thank you Your Honor – I call Bazil Osgood." The jurors gasped. Everyone else was quiet. Bazil stood up, adjusted himself, and walked up to the stand...

"Please state your name for the record..." Judge Duffey instructed...

"Bazil Osgood."

"Please raise your right hand and place your left hand on the bible..." Judge Duffey instructed as the court clerk held the Bible... "Do you swear, under penalty of perjury, that the testimony you are about to give shall be the truth, the whole truth, and nothing but the truth?"

"Absolutely..." Bazil said as he sat down.

"Very well – Beverly – you may proceed…"

"Good afternoon Mr. Osgood…"

"Hello…"

"Do you remember what happened to you on January 13, 2019?"

"I don't remember everything…"

"What do you remember?"

"I remember Sonia was having sex with my wife, I remember joining in… and then I got shot…"

"Are you sure that's what you remember?"

"I remember that…"

'Your Honor – permission to treat the witness as hostile!"

"Permission granted – continue…" Judge Duffey ordered.

"Mr. Osgood – isn't it true that you're merely repeating what your wife told you?"

"Some of it – yes…"

"How can you be sure what she told you is true?"

"My wife loves me – she wouldn't lie about that…" I started crying and Smalls grabbed my hand under the table…

"Is that right?"

"Yes…"

"So – your wife slept with your lover – stabbed you – and left you – but she wouldn't lie to you? Really?"

"My wife loves me – she wouldn't lie to me…"

"Mr. Osgood – I know you love your wife – but you also loved Trevor – isn't that true?"

"Yes..."

"And – based on your wife's testimony – he betrayed you by sleeping with your wife – and – based on your wife's testimony – he shot you – but you loved him – so how can you be sure you wife's telling you the truth?"

"I just am..."

"Mr. Osgood – you've been betrayed by the two people you love most – and yet – you continue to stand by your wife – and she doesn't deserve it..."

"She does!" Bazil snapped as Beverly turned around. Smalls looked at me and grabbed my hand harder to remind me to remain calm but it wasn't working...

"Does she? What did your wife do to earn your devotion?"

"She stayed with me every night I was in a coma – she never left my side..."

"Of course she did - she didn't do that for you – she did that for herself..."

"She made love to me..."

"Oh please – that just means she was horny!" Beverly laughed. Bazil started breathing heavy. His shoulders and his chest started going up and down. His eyes turned to slits... and I was scared. The jury watched and waited...

"When I came out my coma, my wife was there. We made love... and then I died..." Bazil said as he started crying...

"Oh Bazil..." I cried. Smalls pulled me into a hug. The jury was quiet. Troy and Keisha moved closer to the bench...

"You died?" Beverly asked...

"Yes."

"I'm sorry Mr. Osgood – I truly am – but I have to ask – how does this prove your wife loves you?"

"Because... after I died... my wife died..."

"Oh my God!" Keisha said out loud before covering her mouth. The jurors started whispering...

"Your wife died? After you did? How could you possibly know this?"

"Because she followed me..."

"Your wife followed you? Followed you where?"

"My wife followed me to the light..."

"Mr. Osgood – are you sure this wasn't a dream?"

"Yes."

"Okay – I'll entertain you – so your wife followed you to the light – what happened next?"

"I told her to go back but she wouldn't leave me..." he cried. I was crying and I could hear Troy and Keisha crying with me. Smalls was tearing up and so were the jurors...

"Let me get this straight – you died – your wife died – and she followed you?"

"Yes."

"What happened next Mr. Osgood?"

"We saw God..."

"You saw God? Both of you?"

"Yes."

"What happened next?"

"Beautiee begged for my life..." Bazil cried as we all continued crying.

"Your wife begged for your life? Hmmmmm – interesting – continue..."

"God told Beautiee to trust him so she let me go..."

"So - Mr. Osgood – if – as you say – your wife let you go – how are you here?"

"I begged God please don't make Beautiee live without me!" he cried. I saw that Judge Duffey was getting emotional too.

"Mr. Osgood – are you telling the court you asked God to let you come back to your wife – and that's why you're here?"

"Yes..."

"Mr.Osgood – you're an intelligent man – right?"

"Yes..."

"So – let me ask you – isn't it possible that you're here because the doctor revived you?"

"Of course..."

"You love your wife very much – don't you?"

"Yes..."

"You'd do anything to protect her – right?"

"Yes..."

"I have one last question - if it was a matter of life and death – would you lie for her?

Bazil didn't answer right away. Everyone waited for him to answer...

"Yes..."

"I have no further questions – your witness..." Beverly said as she sat down.

"Hey Bazil..." Smalls said as he stood up...

"Hey Smalls..." Bazil said as he smiled.

"You testified that you don't remember everything that happened the night you were shot – right?"

"Yes."

"You also testified you loved Trevor – is that right?"

"Yes."

"Did you ever cut things off with Trevor?"

"Yes."

"How did he feel about that?"

"He begged me not to."

"Did he say why?"

"He begged me not to let my wife come between us..." Keisha and Troy gasped along with the jury.

"But you ended it anyway – didin't you?"

"Yes..."

"Why?"

"Because I didn't want to hurt my wife anymore..." he cried...

"Did that make Trevor angry?"

"I'm not sure..."

"Let me re-phrase the question – isn't it possible that Trevor was angry – just like your wife was angry when she found out about him?"

"Yes... it's possible..."

"So... isn't it also possible that your wife was telling you the truth when she told you that Trevor shot you, shot Sonia, and would have also shot her if she didn't shoot him?"

"It's absolutely possible..."

"Thank you – I have no further questions..." Smalls said as he sat down.

"Please return to the back of the court room..." Judge Duffey said. Bazil got up and went to the back of the court room. Troy and Keisha got up and went to the back of the court room to sit with him.

"Beverly – are you ready to call your next witness?" Judge Duffey asked...

"Yes Your Honor – I call Dr. Ronald Preston." Bazil and I smiled as we watched Dr. Preston took the stand...

"Please state your name for the record..." Judge Duffey instructed...

"Ronald Preston."

"Please raise your right hand and place your left hand on the bible..." Judge Duffey instructed as the court clerk held the Bible... "Do you swear, under penalty of perjury, that the testimony you are about to give shall be the truth, the whole truth, and nothing but the truth?"

"I swear..." Dr. Preston said as he sat down.

"Very well – Beverly – you may proceed..."

"Dr. Preston – what happened on the night Mr. Osgood was brought into the hospital?"

"Mr. Osgood needed emergency surgery. I had to struggle to get the bullet out of him. The surgery went well but when I went to close him up he started coding. His pressure kept dropping so I told him I was trying to get him back to his wife but I needed him to cooperate and relax."

"Do you always talk to your patients when their unconscious?"

"I started talking to my patients after my mother told me she heard everything that was said to her when she was in a coma."

"Go on..."

"I went to see Mrs. Osgood and let her know what happened with her husband during surgery. I explained to her that we had to put him in a medical coma because he lost a lot of blood, his pressure was low, and he was too weak to heal. I didn't think he was going to make it at the time – she asked me what should she do and I told her if she believed in God – she should pray."

"Oh my God!" Troy said. I was crying, Bazil was crying, and Smalls was tearing up along with some of the jurors.

"What happened next?"

"I asked Mrs. Osgood why she was naked."

"What was her response?"

"She said she was having sex with her husband when he got shot. I asked her why she didn't get dressed and she said there wasn't any

14

time, so I asked one of my nurses to get her some pajamas and let her take a shower."

"Was the defendant there every night as Mr. Osgood testified?"

"Yes she was. I've seen a lot of patients with their families and loved ones and I've never seen more dedication and devotion to a patient like I saw with Mrs. Osgood – he's a lucky man." Smalls smiled as Beverly got annoyed...

"Dr. Preston – Mr. Osgood testified that he woke up from his coma – he died – the defendant died – they both saw God – she came back – and he came back – is this true?"

"I can't tell you what happened between them and God because I wasn't there – but what I can tell you is that he died – I tried to revive him but I failed – she died – I was able to revive her – and then he woke up on his own."

"Are you saying you believe they saw God?"

"I'm saying there must be a God because there's no other possible medical explanation for what happened..." Dr. Preston said as he threw up his hands...

"I have no more questions... your witness..." Beverly said as she sat down and shook her head...

"I have no questions for this witness Your Honor..." Smalls said.

"The witness is excused – we're done for today – I'll see everyone tomorrow morning at 9 a.m." Judge Duffey said as he got up from the bench and left. Everyone left the court room except me and Smalls...

"You ready?" Smalls asked...

"No..." I said as I started to cry...

"I know... it's almost over... Bazil's waiting..." he said as he got up to take my hand...

"Okay..." I said as I got up and he walked me into the hallway. Bazil grabbed me as soon as I came out the court room...

"Beautiee... we need to go..." Smalls said as he tugged my arm..."

"Just a few more minutes... please..." I pleaded. Bazil picked up my face and kissed me fully.

"I'll see you tomorrow..." he said before he let me go and left the court house. The Bailiff came over to escort me back to the waiting area with the other prisoners...

"I'll see you first thing tomorrow morning..." Smalls said as he pulled me into a hug...

"Okay..." I sighed...

"Let's go..." the Bailiff said as he took me by the arm. I watched Smalls leave the court house...

"We'll be back tomorrow..." Troy said as Troy and Keisha hugged me together...

"I love y'all..." I said...

"We love you too..." Keisha said before they let me go and then they left the court house. The

Bailiff escorted me back to the waiting area to go back to jail.

Chapter 2

"All rise..."the Bailiff said. Everyone stood up. "Department One of the Superior Court is now in session. Judge Duffey presiding. Please be seated."

"Calling the case of the People of the State of Connecticut versus Beautiee Osgood. Are both sides ready?"

"Ready for the People, Your Honor..." Beverly said.

"Ready for the Defense, Your Honor..." Smalls said.

"Beverly – you may call your next witness..." Judge Duffey said...
"Thank you Your Honor – I call Tisha Andrews."
I watched as Ms. Andrews took the stand...

"Please state your name for the record..." Judge Duffey instructed...

"Tisha Andrews."

"Please raise your right hand and place your left hand on the bible..." Judge Duffey instructed as the court clerk held the Bible... "Do you swear, under penalty of perjury, that the testimony you are about to give shall be the truth, the whole truth, and nothing but the truth?"

"I do..." Tisha said as she sat down.

"Ms. Andrews – please tell the court what happened on January 13, 2019 when the defendant came into the hospital…"

"Mrs. Osgood was distraught. She was covered in blood. She had a robe on but it kept opening. She didn't seem to care that everyone could see her naked body."

"Did you find that odd?"

"Yes I did. I thought it was strange that she didn't take a shower or have clothes on."

"Did you have a conversation with the defendant?"

"Yes I did."

"What did you discuss?"

"I explained to Mrs. Osgood that we needed to do a rape kit, take some pictures, and take some samples."

"How did she react?"

"Mrs. Osgood was angry – she refused to allow me or anyone else to do a rape kit."

"Did you find that odd?"

"Yes I did – if we were able to do a rape kit – we could've determined that she only had sex with her husband and no one else."

"Did you explain that to the defendant?"

"No – I only explained we needed to do a rape kit as a procedure due to the circumstances."

"Did the defendant do a rape kit?"

"No – she refused – she said she wasn't raped."

"I see – were you able to get photos and samples?"

"Yes."

"Your Honor – may I share the photos with the jury?"

"Objection!" Smalls yelled...

"What's your objection Smalls?" Judge Duffey asked...

"Why is it necessary for the jury to see photos of my client naked?"

"Due to the heinous nature of the crimes – I'm sorry – your objection is overruled – Bailiff – please share the photos with the jury." I sat there numb. All I could do was cry. Smalls put his arm around me to comfort me...

"I'm sorry..." he whispered. I watched as the Bailiff passed the photos to the jury – thankfully they weren't too interested – some of the jurors even waived their hand to let the Bailiff know they didn't want to see them. Beverly continued with her questions after the Bailiff returned the photos...

"What was your opinion as you were taking the photos and getting swabs from the defendant?"

"I told Mrs. Osgood I thought she was an angry black woman that shot her husband because she caught him cheating on her..."

"Oh Shit!" Troy said out loud. The jury gasped...

"Thank you – your witness..." Beverly said to Smalls as she sat down...

"Ms. Andrews – you testified that you found it odd that the defendant's robe kept opening – why did you find that odd when you also testified that she appeared to be distraught?"

"People don't normally come to the hospital without getting dressed…"

"Are you comparing the situation with my client to visitors?"

"No… I'm just saying…"

"You're saying that instead of my client staying with her husband because she was afraid he might die – that she should've thought more about taking a shower and getting dressed?"

"Objection – he's badgering the witness!" Beverly snapped…

"Sustained…" Judge Duffey acknowledged…

"Sorry Your Honor – Ms. Andrews – why did you insist on a rape kit when the defendant told you she wasn't raped?"

"As I stated – its procedure in situations like this – it wasn't personal…"

"Isn't it true that rape kits are only procedure when someone says they've been raped?"

"Normally – yes – but nothing about this was normal!"

"Exactly – you also testified that you told the defendant you thought she was an angry black woman that shot her husband because she caught him cheating on her – what made you think that?"

"Because she was covered in blood…"

"Isn't it possible that the defendant was covered in blood due to blood splatter?"

"Yes it is..."

"Isn't it also possible that the blood could've gotten on the defendant because she held her husband close to her?"

"Yes – it's possible..."

"It's not just possible – it's probable – no further questions..." Smalls said as he sat down...

"Beverly – you may call your next witness..." Judge Duffey ordered...

"Thank you Your Honor – I call Mr. A. Grady – the Coroner from the Fairfield County Medical Examiner's Office.

"Please state your name for the record..." Judge Duffey instructed...

"Mr. A. Grady."

"Please raise your right hand and place your left hand on the bible..." Judge Duffey instructed as the court clerk held the Bible... "Do you swear, under penalty of perjury, that the testimony you are about to give shall be the truth, the whole truth, and nothing but the truth?"

"I do..." Mr. Grady said as he sat down.

"Mr. Grady – on January 13, 2019 – did you perform the autopsies on Sonia Santos and Trevor Joseph?"

"Yes I did."

"Please tell the court what you determined to be the cause of death during the autopsies..."

"The cause of death for Sonia Santos was a single shot in the back under the right shoulder blade. The cause of death for Trevor Joseph was a single shot to the chest. Both victims were shot within close range."

"How were you able to determine this?"

"I was able to determine that by the depth of the bullet penetration into each of the bodies."

"Could you please explain?"

"We take two radiographs at 90 degrees to each other to estimate the depth of the bullet in the body. Once we determine the depth of the bullet into the body, we place bullets of different calibers alongside the body at a suitable position and then image them to compare the bullet caliber."

"Did you examine the bullet removed from Mr. Osgood?"

"Yes I did."

"What did you find?"

"The bullet removed from Mr. Osgood was a perfect match to the bullets removed from Sonia Santos and Trevor Joseph."

"Thank you – your witness..." Beverly said to Smalls as she sat down...

"Mr. Grady..." Smalls asked as he stood up... "You testified that both Sonia Santos and Trevor Joseph were shot in close range – is that correct?"

"Yes."

"And you testified that Sonia Santos was shot in the back – right?"

"Yes."

"In your opinion – if both victims were close to the defendant – wouldn't one of them have jumped to the side to avoid being shot?"

"Not necessarily..."

"Please explain..."

"Well – if the defendant had the gun pointed at them and told them not to move – they might not have moved – it's possible the defendant may have told them to put their hands up and don't move..."

"Mr. Grady – do you see the defendant here in the court room?"

"Yes."

"And do you also see the defendant's husband in the court room?"

"Yes I do."

"And – since you performed the autopsies – both Sonia Santos and Trevor Joseph are taller and larger than the defendant – right?"

"Yes."

"So – do you really think it's possible that my client held her husband – held Sonia – and held Trevor – at gun point – then shot all three of them – and they just stood there with their hands up – without a struggle – and no one tried to get the gun away from her?" The Coroner hesitated before answering...

"Well... since you put it that way... no..." The jurors started whispering. Bazil and I smiled.

"Thank you – no further questions..." Smalls said as he sat down.

"The witness is excused." Judge Duffy waited for Mr. Grady to leave the stand before continuing... "Does the prosecution rest?"

"Yes Your Honor..." Beverly answered.

"Does the defense rest?"

"Yes Your Honor..." Smalls answered.

"Are you ready with final arguments?" Judge Duffey asked...

"Yes Your Honor..." Beverly answered.

"Yes Hour Honor..." Smalls answered.

"Very well – you may begin..." Judge Duffey said. Beverly went first...

Chapter 3

Beverly's Closing Argument

"Ladies and gentlemen of the jury,

You've heard a lot of testimony. You've seen a lot of evidence. As you go into deliberations, I want you to remember the defendant's testimony. She testified she caught her husband cheating on her. She testified she slept with her husband's lover to hurt him. She testified she stabbed him. She testified she left him. She testified she invited Sonia Santos over for her husband to watch them have sex and later join in – but the truth is – she set them both up along with Trevor Joseph. She testified she didn't invite Trevor into their home – but how can we believe that when she slept with him? And yes – we've seen a lot of affection between these two – but don't believe for one second that the defendant loves her husband – he definitely loves her – but she doesn't love anyone but herself – she's doing what she does – whatever it takes to protect her own interests. The defendant had reason, motive, and opportunity to get them all – and she executed it perfectly – well... almost perfectly. When you're done with your deliberations – return with a verdict of 'Guilty' on all counts. Thank you."

Small's Closing Argument

"Ladies and gentlemen of the jury,

I agree with the prosecution – you should remember the defendant's testimony. Yes – she did testify that her husband cheated on her – and yes – she testified she slept with her husband's lover to hurt him – because she was hurt. Yes – she did testify she stabbed her husband – in his hand! If she were trying to kill her husband – she would have stabbed in in the heart, the chest, the neck – even his back! No one has ever died from being stabbed in the hand! Yes – she also testified she left him – again – if she wanted to kill him – he wouldn't have been able to walk out the house before she left! Yes – she testified she invited Sonia Santos over for her husband to watch them have sex and later join in – since when is having a threesome a crime? In spite of what the prosecution wants you to think – Trevor Joseph was not invited to their home. Yes – the defendant slept with him – but that is not an invitation to come over and the prosecution didn't prove otherwise! And yes – we've all witnessed the genuine affection between the defendant and her husband. I have no doubt whatsoever that the love between them is real – and neither should you. The prosecution would have you believe the defendant had reason – yes she did have reason – she had reason to leave her husband – and she left her husband – but she went back to her husband because she loves her husband – she didn't go back to her husband to kill him! And yes – the defendant had reason and motive to invite Sonia Santos over to their home – and that reason and motive was sex – not murder – and remember – according to the Coroner's testimony – Sonia was shot in the back – how was the defendant able to shoot her husband – then turn around and shoot Sonia in the back unless Sonia turned her back on the defendant – and – if the defendant was responsible for the gun – once she shot her husband – neither Sonia nor Trevor would turn their back on the defendant – let alone stand still and wait to be shot! My client has been through too much already. When you're done with your deliberations – return with a verdict of 'Not Guilty' on all counts. Thank you."

"Ladies and gentlemen of the jury, I am now going to read to you the law that you must follow in deciding this case…" Judge Duffey said as he stood up and began reading:

COURT'S STANDARD INSTRUCTIONS TO THE JURY IN A CRIMINAL TRIAL

"It is my duty to instruct you on the rules of law that you must use in deciding this case. After I've completed these instructions, you will go to the jury room and begin your discussions or what we call your deliberations in this case. You must decide whether the Government has proved beyond a reasonable doubt the specific facts necessary to find the Defendant guilty of the crimes charged in the indictment."

DUTY TO FOLLOW INSTRUCTIONS PRESUMPTION OF INNOCENCE

"Your decision must be based only on the evidence presented here. You must not be influenced in any way by either sympathy or prejudice for or against the Defendant or the Government. You must also follow the law as I explain it, even if you do not agree with the law. And, you must follow all of my instructions as a whole. You may not single out, or disregard, any of my instructions on the law. The indictment or formal charges against a defendant is not evidence of guilt. The law presumes that every defendant is innocent. The Defendant does not have to prove her innocence or produce any evidence at all. The Government must prove guilt beyond a reasonable doubt, and if it fails to do so you must find the Defendant not guilty."

DEFINITION OF REASONABLE DOUBT

"While the Government's burden of proof is a heavy one, the Government does not have to prove a defendant's guilt beyond all possible doubt. The Government's proof only has to exclude any "reasonable doubt" concerning the Defendant's guilt. A "reasonable doubt" is a real doubt, based upon your reason and common sense, after you've carefully and impartially considered all the evidence in the case. "Proof beyond a reasonable doubt," is proof so convincing that you would be willing to rely and act on it, without hesitation, in the most important of your own affairs. If you are convinced that the Defendant has been proved guilty beyond a reasonable doubt, say so. If you are not convinced, say so."

CONSIDERATION OF THE EVIDENCE, DIRECT AND CIRCUMSTANTIAL-- ARGUMENT OF COUNSEL COMMENTS BY THE COURT

"As I mentioned earlier, you must consider only the evidence that I admitted in the case. 'Evidence' includes the testimony of witnesses and the exhibits admitted during the trial. Remember, anything the lawyers say is not evidence in the case and it isn't binding on you. Your own recollection and interpretation of the evidence is what matters. You should not assume from anything I may have said that I have any opinion about any factual issues in this case. Except for my instructions to you on the law, [and any limiting instructions I gave regarding your consideration of certain evidence,] you should disregard anything I may have said during the trial in arriving at your own decision concerning the facts. In considering the evidence, you may use reason and common sense to make deductions and to reach conclusions. You should not be concerned about whether the evidence is direct or circumstantial. Court's Standard Instructions to the Jury (Criminal) 6 "Direct evidence" is the testimony of a person who asserts that he or she has actual knowledge of a fact, such as an eye witness. "Circumstantial evidence" is proof of a chain of facts and circumstances tending to prove, or disprove, a fact. There is no legal difference in the weight you may give to either direct or circumstantial evidence."

CREDIBILITY OF WITNESSES

"When I say you must consider all of the evidence, I do not mean that you must accept all of the evidence as true or accurate. You should decide whether you believe what each witness had to say, and the importance of that testimony. In making that decision you may believe or disbelieve any witness, in whole or in part. Also, the number of witnesses testifying concerning any particular point doesn't necessarily matter. To decide whether you believe any witness I suggest that you ask yourself a few questions: 1. Did the witness impress you as one who was telling the truth? 2. Did the witness have any particular reason not to tell the truth? 3. Did the witness have a personal interest in the outcome of the case? 4. Did the witness have a bias or prejudice? 5. Did the witness seem to have a good memory? 6. Did the witness have the opportunity and ability to observe accurately the things about which he or she testified? 7. Did the witness appear to understand the questions clearly and answer them directly? 8. Did the witness's testimony differ from other testimony or other evidence? 9. What was the witness's demeanor while testifying? 10. Any other facts that affect the witness's credibility."

IMPEACHMENT INCONSISTENT STATEMENT

"You should also ask yourself whether there was evidence that a witness testified falsely about an important fact. And ask whether there was evidence that, at some other time, a witness said or did something, or didn't say or do something, that was different from the testimony the witness gave during this trial. But keep in mind that a simple mistake does not mean a witness was not telling the truth as he or she remembers it, because people naturally tend to forget some things or remember them inaccurately. If a witness misstated something, you must decide whether it was because of an innocent lapse in memory or an intentional deception. The significance of your decision may depend on whether the misstatement is about an important fact or about an unimportant detail."

DEFENDANT TESTIFIES WITH NO FELONY CONVICTION

"A defendant has a right not to testify. Since the defendant did testify in this case, you should decide whether you believe the defendant's testimony in the same way you evaluated the credibility of any other witness."

EXPERT WITNESSES

"Expert testimony was admitted in this case. When scientific, technical, or other specialized knowledge might be helpful in a case, a person who has special training or experience in a particular field is allowed to state an opinion about the matter. That does not mean that you must accept the expert witness's opinion. As with any other witness, you must decide the extent to which, if any, to rely upon the opinion offered."

INTRODUCTION TO SPECIFIC OFFENSE INSTRUCTION

"The indictment charges separate crimes, called 'counts' against the Defendant. You will be given a copy of the indictment to refer to the charges during your deliberations. To find the Defendant guilty of any of the counts charged in the indictment, the government must prove to you beyond a reasonable doubt that the Defendant committed each element of the offense."

ON OR ABOUT

"You will see that the indictment charges that a crime was committed "on or about" a certain date. The Government does not have to prove that the crime occurred on an exact date. The Government only has to prove beyond a reasonable doubt that the crime was committed on a date reasonably close to the date alleged."

KNOWINGLY AND WILLFULLY AND SPECIFIC INTENT

"The word 'knowingly' means that an act was done voluntarily and intentionally, and not because of mistake or by accident. The word 'willfully' means that the act was committed voluntarily and purposely, with the intent to do something the law forbids; that is with the bad purpose to disobey or disregard the law. While a person must have acted with the intent to do something the law forbids before you can find that the person acted "willfully," the person need not be aware of the specific law or rule that their conduct may be violating."

CAUTION – PUNISHMENT (SINGLE DEFENDANT – MULTIPLE COUNTS)

"Each count of the indictment charges a separate crime. You must consider each crime and the evidence relating to it considered separately. If you find the Defendant guilty or not guilty of one crime, that must not affect your verdict for any other crime. I caution you that the Defendant is on trial only for those specific crimes charged in the indictment. You are here to determine from the evidence in this case whether the Defendant is guilty or not guilty of these specific crimes. You must not consider punishment in any way in deciding whether the Defendant is guilty or not guilty. If you find the Defendant guilty, the punishment is for me alone to decide later."

DUTY TO DELIBERATE

"Your verdict, whether guilty or not guilty, must be unanimous – in other words, you must all agree. Your deliberations are secret; and you will never have to explain your verdict to anyone. You must discuss the case with one another to try to reach agreement. Each of you must decide the case for yourself, but only after fully considering the evidence with the other jurors. While you are discussing the case, do not hesitate to reexamine your own opinions and change your mind if you become convinced that you were wrong. But do not give up your honest beliefs just because the others think differently, or simply because you want to conclude the case. Remember that in a very real way you are judges – judges of the facts. Your only interest is to seek the truth from the evidence in this case. During your deliberations, you must not communicate with or provide any information to anyone by any means about this case. You may not use any electronic device or media, such as a telephone, cell or Court's Standard Instructions to the Jury (Criminal) 23 smart phone, Blackberry or computer, the internet, or any messaging service to communicate to anyone any information about this case, or to conduct any research about this case until I accept your verdict."

FOREPERSON AND PROCEDURE

"When you get to the jury room you should choose one of your members to act as foreperson. The foreperson will direct your deliberations and will speak for you in court. A verdict form has been prepared for your convenience. Take the verdict form with you to the jury room. When you have all agreed on the verdict, your foreperson must fill in the form, sign it and date it, and advise the Court Security Officer that you have reached a verdict. He will notify me so we can reconvene in the courtroom. If you wish to communicate with me at any time, please write down your message, or question, and give it to the Court Security Officer who will bring it to my attention. I will respond as soon as possible, either in writing or by talking to you in the courtroom. But I caution you – do not disclose in your notes or in court to me how many jurors have voted one way or the other."

"These are your instructions. You will now go to the jury room but do not begin your deliberations until you receive the exhibits and I tell you that your deliberations may begin."

Jury Deliberations

"Damn – I'm glad they wouldn't let me out of Jury Duty – this has been the best two weeks of my life! Too bad we can't talk about this shit when it's over!" Female Juror #6 said...

"I can' wait to get back to work – all my co-workers hated Jury Duty – they all got boring cases – they gonna be hatin'!" Female Juror #7 laughed...

"Personally, I can't wait to get this over with – I'm ready to get back to my boring life..." Male Juror #8 said...

"Boring life?" Male Juror #9 asked...

"I used to beg my wife to try something new – spice it up a little – but after listening to all this testimony – I'm glad my wife refused..." Male Juror #8 said...

"Well... my wife and I have tried a few things... but we've never invited anyone else into the bedroom..." Male Juror #9 said...

"Why not? Don't you want a threesome with another woman?" Female Juror #10 asked...

"I'd love one – but my wife wants another man – and just like Bazil – I ain't havin' that shit!" Male Juror #9 snapped...

"Typical male bullshit – you cool wit' it as long as she wants another woman 'cause you can have your cake and eat it too – but no man is ever okay with his wife having another man!" Female Juror #10 snapped...

"Why the hell would I be okay with that shit? I'm not gay – what the fuck am I supposed to do while he's fuckin' my wife – jerk off?" Male Juror #9 snapped...

"You could do that... if you wanted to..." Male Juror #12 said...

"Really? Are you serious right now? I'm not gay!" Male Juror #9 yelled...

"Why are you taking this personal? I'm just saying..." Male Juror #12 said...

"What the fuck are you just saying? You and your wife do that shit?" Male Juror #9 snapped...

"That's exactly what I'm saying..." male Juror #12 said...

"How can you jerk off to another man... unless you're gay?" Male Juror #9 asked...

"I'm not jerking off to another man per sey... I'm turned on by my wife enjoying herself..." Male Juror #12 answered...

"See – that's what I'm talkin' about!" Female Juror #10 said...

"Why are we talkin' about this anyway? Personally, I'd rather not hear all about your personal conquests..." Male Juror #2 said...

"Well... to answer your question... we're all talkin' about this because it is what it is – we're all adults, we're all fuckin' – some of us are fuckin' one person – some of us are fuckin' more than one person – but we're all doing it!" Male Juror #4 explained...

"Exactly!" Female Juror #1 agreed...

"I think she got exactly what she deserved – she said she slept with her husband's lover because she wanted to hurt him – ain't that much hate in the world – if my husband cheated on me with a man I'd leave him – not fuck the same man my husband was fuckin' – she did that shit 'cause she wanted him from the beginning – she just used her husband fuckin' him first as an excuse!" Female Juror #3 snapped...

"I was thinking the same thing..." Female Juror #11 agreed...

"That doesn't make her a murder..." Male Juror #5 said...

"No... it doesn't make her a murdered... but I ain't mad if she did – I would'a killed my husband too!" Female Juror #1 said...

"So – you think she's guilty?" male Juror #2 asked...

"I'm not sure – maybe she did shoot him – but from what I've seen – from what we've all seen – she loves her husband..." Female Juror #1 answered...

"I was ready to run to the witness stand and hug her husband when he said he died and then she died and followed him to the light..." Female Juror #3 said...

"You actually fell for that – poor thing – he was in a coma – it was a dream!" Male Juror #4 laughed...

"I believe it happened just like he said..." Male Juror #5 said...

"Why do you believe it?" Female Juror #6 asked...

"Because the doctor confirmed it..." Male Juror #5 answered...

"All he said was there was no other medical explanation..." Female Juror #6 said...

"I don't think she shot her husband – I think she's crazy – crazy enough to invite another woman into her bed to satisfy her husband's fantasy..." Female Juror #7 said...

"That was her fantasy just as much as it was his – trust me – I know..." Male Juror #8 said...

"I thought you said your life was boring?" Male Juror #9 asked...

"It is – and since this trial started – I thank God for it every day..." Male Juror #8 answered...

"I hear ya – I've been thanking God everyday too – my husband appreciates all the affection he's been getting from me lately..." Female Juror #10 said...

"This trial definitely puts things in perspective..." Female Juror #11 said...

"There wouldn't be a trial in the first place if her husband didn't push her over the edge..." Male Juror #12 said...

"So – it seems like we're all in agreement that she's not guilty of trying to kill her husband – right?" Male Juror #2 asked...

"Who made you the foreperson?" Male Juror #4 asked...

"Sigh... it doesn't matter to me one way or the other..." Male Juror #2 answered...

"Well – I think we should vote on it..." Male Juror #4 said...

"I'm fine with him being the foreperson..." Female Juror #1 said...

"I'm fine with it too – anyone else want to do it – or have any objections?" Male Juror #2 asked...

"Fine with me..." Female Juror #3 said...

"Sigh... okay..." Male Juror #4 said...

"I'm fine with it..." Male Juror #5 said...

"I'm fine with it..." Female Juror #6 said...

"I'm fine with it – and you're fine too..." Female Juror #7 said as she smiled...

"Thank you for your vote... and the compliment..." Male Juror #2 said as he smiled...

"I'm fine with it..." Male Juror #8 said...

"I'm fine with it..." Male Juror #9 said...

"I'm fine with it..." Female Juror #10 said...

"I'm fine with it..." Female Juror #11 said...

"I'm fine with it too..." Male Juror #12 said...

"Thank you all for that. Let me add – I promise to listen to everybody – I don't necessarily want to know all your business – but if you choose to tell it – I'll hear it – don't be mad if I take notes – I may be an old dog but I'm open to learning new tricks..." Male Juror #2 said. All the jurors bust out laughing... "So – are we all in agreement that the defendant is not guilty of the attempted murder of her husband? I'll start with myself – Not Guilty..."

"Not Guilty..." Female Juror #1 answered...

"Not Guilty..." Female Juror #3 answered...

"Not Guilty..." Male Juror #4 answered...

"Not Guilty..." Male Juror #5 answered...

"Not Guilty..." Female Juror #6 answered...

"Not Guilty..." Female Juror #7 answered...

"Not Guilty..." Male Juror #8 answered...

"Not Guilty..." Male Juror #9 answered...

"Not Guilty..." Female Juror #10 answered...

"Not Guilty..." Female Juror #11 answered...

"Not Guilty..." Male Juror #12 answered...

"Okay – now how do we all feel about Sonia Santos? Did the defendant invite Sonia over to have sex because she was setting Sonia up to be killed or was it just to have a good-ole fashioned threesome? Personally – I think it was to have a good-ole fashioned threesome..." Male Juror #2 said...

"I think it was a good-ole fashioned threesome too – but how did she meet Sonia anyway?" Female Juror #1 asked...

"Why is that significant?" Male Juror #2 asked...

"Why would Trevor shoot her?" Female Juror #1 asked...

"According to the defendant's testimony – Trevor was aiming at the both of them – when Sonia got shot – Trevor blamed the defendant and said Sonia wasn't supposed to die – I think they both set the defendant up and it backfired..." Male Juror #2 answered...

"Maybe they did – but the defendant's fingerprints are on the gun so we have no way of knowing for sure..." Female Juror #1 said...

"Can we just call the defendant by her name? It's not like we don't know it..." Female Juror #3 said...

"I don't care what we call her — do you think she's guilty of killing Sonia?" Male Juror #2 asked...

"No — I think she got what she deserved for cheating on her husband with Trevor — but I don't think she's guilty of killing Sonia..." Female Juror #3 answered...

"Excuse me — how can you blame the defendant — Beautiee — for that man coming into her home and trying to kill her and her husband? So what she had sex with him — her husband had sex with him first — maybe it's like Beautiee said — he was angry because her husband chose her over him and he didn't wanna lose the dick — good dick make's a man crazy too ya know..." Male Juror #4 laughed...

"How would you know?" Female Juror #3 asked...

"After listening to all this testimony — I have no doubt that's what happened..." Male Juror #4 answered...

"I don't think she deserved what happened to her — but I do think she's responsible for opening the door..." Male Juror #5 said...

"That's what I'm saying!" Female Juror #3 agreed...

"I feel sorry for Beautiee — all she wanted was her husband — her husband is a mutha-fucka for puttin' her through this shit — it should 'a been him on trial — not her!" Female Juror #6 snapped...

"I agree! And besides — like her attorney said — having a threesome isn't a crime..." Female Juror #7 said...

"It may not be a crime — but it damn sure has consequences!" Male Juror #8 said...

"As long as it's consensual — it works..." male Juror #9 said...

"I think Trevor consented with everything until Bazil chose his wife..." Female Juror #10 said...

"Me too..." Female Juror #11 agreed...

"If Beautiee chose my wife instead of Sonia... things would 'a damn sure turned out different..." Male Juror #12 said...

"Reallly? Jackass!" Male Juror #4 snapped...

"Who you calling jackass?" male Juror #12 snapped...

"You – 'cause you're a jackass – this woman's life is on the line – and all you can think about is a threesome with her?" Male Juror #2 asked...

"Well... since you asked... to be honest... yes... and I'm probably not the only one... but that was crude... sorry..." Male Juror #12 answered...

"Sigh... Anyway – do we all agree that Beautiee isn't guilty of killing Sonia? I'll start with myself – Not Guilty..."

"Not Guilty..." Female Juror #1 answered...
"Not Guilty..." Female Juror #3 answered...

"Not Guilty..." Male Juror #4 answered...

"Not Guilty..." Male Juror #5 answered...

"Not Guilty..." Female Juror #6 answered...

"Not Guilty..." Female Juror #7 answered...

"Not Guilty..." Male Juror #8 answered...

"Not Guilty..." Male Juror #9 answered...

"Not Guilty..." Female Juror #10 answered...

"Not Guilty..." Female Juror #11 answered...

"Not Guilty..." Male Juror #12 answered...

"Good... moving right along... what does everyone think about Beautiee killing Trevor?" Male Juror #2 asked...

"Guilty..." Female Juror #1 answered...

'Why?" Male Juror #2 asked...

"It doesn't matter..." Female Juror #1 answered...

"It matters to me because I don't think she's guilty – I want to hear what you have to say about it..." Male Juror #2 said...

"I understand he shot her husband – so she says – but she also says he dropped the gun – he ran to Sonia – he pulled her up and hugged her – he was distraught – how can we be sure he was going to pick up the gun again?" Female Juror #1 asked...

"You have a valid point..." Male Juror #2 answered...

"I agree – I think Beautiee saw an opportunity for revenge and she took it – the fact that he shot her husband give her a self-defense claim – but how do we know he intended to pick the gun back up after crying over Sonia?" Female Juror #3 asked...

"I feel the same way – I understand he shot her husband – but once he dropped the gun to cry for Sonia – how can we be sure he intended to pick the gun back up?" male Juror #4 asked...

"I also think in that moment she saw an opportunity for revenge and took it..." Male Juror #5 said...

"I would'a wanted revenge too – and I would'a got it – by any means necessary – just like she did..." Female Juror #6 said...

"Yea – if he shot my husband and dropped the gun –he would'a had to die..." Female Juror #7 said...

"I can only imagine what I would've done if it were my wife – I would've picked up that gun and shot him whether I was threatened or not – and she did..." Male Juror #8 said...

"I know... damn shame... but I agree... I'm not so sure he was going to pick up that gun again and shoot her..." Male Juror #9 said...

"Damn – this is hard – I wanna say I believe her... but he dropped the gun... she could've kicked it outta the way or under the bed..." Female Juror #10 said...

"She could'a thrown the gun instead of shooting him..." Female Juror #11 said...

"She could've thrown the gun – but she didn't – either way, her fingerprints were on it – and if she didn't shoot Trevor he would've testified against her anyway – but she shot him – I understand it... but it's still murder..." Male Juror #12 said...

"I can't believe I'm saying this – but you all have valid points. I don't think she's guilty but I'm not one hundred percent convinced she's innocent of this one – I'm changing my vote to Guilty..." Male Juror #2 said...

"Guilty..." Female Juror #1 answered...

"Guilty..." Female Juror #3 answered...

"Guilty..." Male Juror #4 answered...

"Guilty..." Male Juror #5 answered...

"Guilty..." Female Juror #6 answered...

"Guilty..." Female Juror #7 answered...

"Guilty..." Male Juror #8 answered...

"Guilty..." Male Juror #9 answered...

"Guilty..." Female Juror #10 answered...

"Guilty..." Female Juror #11 answered...

"Guilty..." Male Juror #12 answered...

"Now that we're done with the deliberations – here's my phone number – call me sooner rather than later..." Female Juror #7 said...

"Thank you..." Male Juror #2 said as he put the phone number in his pocket... "I will..." After he put the phone number in his pocket, he wrote the verdict on the verdict form and passed it around the table for all the jurors to sign. After everyone signed it, he picked it up and opened the door... "We're ready..." he said to the Court Security Officer. The Court Security Officer notified Judge Duffey as the Bailiff escorted the jurors back into the jury box. We all watched as the Bailiff handed the form to the court clerk. The court clerk stood up and began reading:

"On the Charge of Attempted Murder in the First Degree of Bazil Osgood – we, the jury, find the defendant...Not Guilty!"

"Yes!" Troy said behind us before putting his hand over his mouth. Smalls smiled, Bazil and I clung to each other, and Beverly shook her head...

"On the Charge of Murder in the First Degree of Sonia Santos – we, the jury, find the defendant... Not Guilty!"

"Thank you Lord..." Keisha whispered. Smalls looked over at Beverly, taunting her with an even bigger Smile, Bazil pulled me into a kiss, and Beverly sat down and folded her arms in defeat...

"On the Charge of Murder in the First Degree of Trevor Joseph – we, the jury, find the defendant...Guilty!" Beverly stood up from the table and looked directly as Smalls with a 'Finally Gotchu Mutha Fucka' look on her face. Smalls shook his head, sighed, turned to me and whispered...

"I'm sorry..." Bazil and I clung to each other as tears streamed down our faces...

"Yo – that's fucked up..." Troy said as he choked up. Keisha pulled him into a hug as he started crying...

"Foreman of the Jury please stand..." Judge Duffey ordered. Male Juror #2 stood up...

"Is the verdict correct?"

"Yes your honor..." Male Juror #2 sighed...

"Bailiff – please give the attorney's an opportunity to examine the verdict form." Beverly examined the form first. She tried not to gloat as she held it in her hand but she couldn't contain her excitement. The Bailiff took the verdict form and brought it to Smalls. Smalls snatched the form, looked at it, and threw it down on the table. The Bailiff went to pick it up but Bazil snatched it up to read it before the Bailiff could...

"Bazil..." Smalls whispered as he touched Bazil's hand..."

"This isn't right... there must be some mistake..." Bazil cried... "Your Honor... please... take me..."

"Mr. Osgood... please give the form to the Bailiff..." Judge Duffey ordered. Bazil handed the form to the Bailiff, the Bailiff handed the form back to the court clerk, and then Judge Duffey spoke...

"Very well..." Judge Duffey sighed... "The jury is dismissed. Thank you for your service." The Bailiff opened the door to the waiting room and escorted the jury out the waiting room through another exit. When the Bailiff returned

to the court room Judge Duffey spoke again...
"Will the defendant, Beautiee Osgood, please
rise." I stood up but my legs began to tremble.
Bazil stood up and held on to me for dear life...
"On the Charge of Attempted Murder in the First
Degree of your husband – Bazil Osgood – you
have been found Not Guilty. On the Charge of
Murder in the First Degree of Sonia Santos – you
have been found Not Guilty. On the Charge of
Murder in the First Degree of Trevor Joseph –
you have been found Guilty – however – based on
the testimony – it is the opinion of this court that
the prosecution failed to prove you had intention
of killing Trevor Joseph with malice or contempt.
It is also the opinion of this court that since your
fingerprints were the only fingerprints on the gun
and all three victims were shot by the same gun –
you can't possibly be guilty of murdering one
victim without also being guilty of murdering the
other victim and attempting to murder your
husband - therefore – I'm setting aside the Guilty
Verdict and entering a judgement of acquittal..."
he said and then he banged the gavel for
emphasis. "Mrs. Osgood – you're free to go."
Beverly threw up her hands and fell back in the
chair. Smalls stood up, chest out, smiling,
fighting back tears...

"Oh shit! That's what I'm talkin' about!"
Troy said as he hugged Keisha and they jumped
up and down. Bazil and I were kissing like
nobody else was in the court room...

"Mrs. Osgood?" Judge Duffey interrupted...

"Yes Your Honor?"

"I said you're free to go…" he laughed…

"Oh – right…" I said as I let go of Bazil and ran to the bench…

"You're going the wrong way…" Judge Duffey laughed as he pointed in the opposite direction…

"Thank you…" I cried as I threw my arms around his neck and hugged him…

"Smalls – come get your client before I change my damn mind…" he laughed. I let go, ran back to Bazil, and jumped into his arms, knocking him down on the floor. Everyone bust out laughing…

"C'mon y'all…" Smalls laughed as he helped me up, and then Bazil…

"Let's go!" Bazil said as he snatched me by the hand and pulled me out the court room…

Chapter 4

"Where we goin'?" I asked... running to keep up...

"Follow me..." he said as he ran out the court house and I followed him across the street to the Holiday Inn...

"Mr. Osgood — nice to see you..." the clerk said as she put his card on the counter...

"You're all set..." she said as she handed Bazil the keys, he snatched my hand again, and pulled me towards the elevator. When the elevator doors opened, Bazil pulled me inside, pushed me against the back, and held his body against me as he kissed me. The bell rang, the door opened, and Bazil pulled me out the elevator and down the hall towards our room. When we got to our room, Bazil got the key, swiped it, opened the door, pulled me inside the room, and closed the door. Bazil continued kissing me as he unzipped the prison jumpsuit, slid it off my shoulders, and let it drop to the floor. I stood there and watched him take off his clothes until he was standing in front of me completely nude. Bazil took me by the hand, led me into the bathroom, and turned on the shower. As the water got hot, he took my hand, led me into the shower, wrapped his arm around me, pulled me into a kiss, and held me against him as we continued kissing. I could feel his dick pressing against me so I reached down to grab it and started stroking it as Bazil reach down to play with my pussy. We continued kissing and playing with each other and moaned in each other's mouths as we came together...

"MmmmMmmm...   MmmmMmmm.....
MmmmMmmm..."
"Mmmmmph...   Mmmmmph...
Mmmmmph..."

Bazil soaped up the washcloth and washed me all over, taking his time on my breasts and between my legs. He turned me around and washed my back and my ass while pulling me close to him and kissing me on my neck. He turned me around to face him and I returned the favor, washing him all over, taking my time as he kissed me. When I reached his dick and his balls, I washed them with my hands and stroked him until he was hard again. I washed his back and his ass as Bazil pulled me closer and continued kissing me. Bazil turned off the water and led me out the shower. He stood me in front of the mirror so I could watch him dry me off while he stood in back of me, kissing me on my neck. When he finished drying me off, he dropped the towel, pushed me forward, spread my legs, and slid himself inside me. I watched us in the mirror as he pulled me to him and began fucking me from behind...

"Oh Bazil..." I moaned as I braced myself on the counter and continued watching us in the mirror...

"Yes... Beautiee..." Bazil moaned as I watched him breathe in my ear and kiss my neck..."

"I'm cumming Bazil..." I moaned as I continued to watch us in the mirror...

"I'm cumming with you..." he moaned as I watched him grab my shoulders and I felt him fucking me harder...

"Bazil!!! I'm cummmmiiiinnnnggg!!!"

"Cum for me!!!" he growled as he fucked me harder and faster... and I saw my breasts swing back and forth in the mirror...

"Aaagggggghhhhhh!"

"Uuuugggghhhh!   Uuuuugggghhhhh! Uuuugggghhhhh!!!"

I continued watching us in the mirror as Bazil kissed me on my neck and shoulders until he turned me around to face him, pulled me close to him, and kissed me fully. Bazil stopped kissing me, took me by the hand, and led me to bed. He turned back the covers and the sheets, climbed into bed, and I climbed in beside him, and lay on his chest as he wrapped his arm around me... and I started to cry...

"Excuse me..." Smalls said to Male Juror #2 to get his attention...

"Yes Sir?" he acknowledged...

"May I ask you a question?"

"Sure..."

"Well... if you don't mind me saying... when Judge Duffey asked you if the verdict was correct... it seemed as if you hesitated...

"I did..." he acknowledged...

"I thought so. Do you mind telling me why?"

"You're not going to report me to the judge right?"

"Oh no... it's over anyway... I just want to know..."

"You're sure? I won't get in any trouble?"

"You have my word..."

"Okay..." he sighed... "I hesitated because I'm not sure she's guilty..."

"So why'd you sign the verdict form that she's guilty if you weren't sure?"

"Well... I listened to everyone else's opinion... and their arguments were compelling..."

"Hmmmm... okay... thank you for telling me... I appreciate that..."

"You're welcome – hey – can I ask you something?"

"Sure..."

"Is she gonna be okay?"

"Yea..."

"I sure wish I could find out what's going to happen to her..."

"You can – it's public record – go to the office downstairs – give them the case name – and ask them to tell you what the sentence was – or you can go on-line and print it out in a couple of days..." Smalls said with a smile...

"Thanks..."

"You're welcome..." Smalls said as he left the court house...

"What's wrong... please don't cry..." Bazil whispered as he started crying with me...

"How could you still love me?" I cried...

"Beautiee..." he whispered before pulling me into a kiss... "How could you still love me?"

"After everything I've done..."

"Please..." he said as he kissed my tears... "I'm the one... it wasn't you... it was me..."

"I wish I never slept with Trevor..."

"I should've ended it as soon as I married you..."

"I should've just left you..."

"You did..."

"I mean... I never should've gone to the hotel..."

"Beautiee... please stop..." Bazil cried...

"I can't help it..."

"I've hurt you so much... I promised God I'd never hurt you again... and I broke that promise..." Bazil said as he cried even harder...

"No... my Thirst Quencher..." I whispered before pulling him into a kiss... "You've kept that promise..." I said before kissing him again... "Ever since you've come back to me... you haven't done anything to hurt me... please stop crying..." I said as I continued to cry...

"I'll stop if you will..." he said as we continued kissing...

"Okay..." I said as he pulled me close to him and pulled me down on the bed...

"Sing to me..." he said and then he started kissing me on my neck...

"'Bout time you got here – hurry up – this shit is heavy!" Keisha said when she saw Smalls getting out of the car...

"Alright – I'm coming..." he said as he got the keys out and opened the door...

"Whew – thank God!" Keisha said as she put the tray of baked ziti down on the counter...

"Open the door!" Troy yelled...

"I'm coming' Babe..." Keisha said as she ran to open the door...

"Whew – thanks Babe..." Troy said as he kissed her...

"You need help?" Smalls asked...

"Yea..." Troy answered as he brought the six foot wedge into the kitchen and placed it on the counter. Smalls held the door open as Troy went back to the car and brought in a couple of 2-liter bottles of Pepsi and ginger ale. After placing those on the counter, Keisha held the door open as Smalls and Troy went out to the car and came back with two cases of Heineken...

"Damn – who drinkin' all that?" she asked...

"We are!" Troy and Smalls said in unison. Keisha looked out the door to see Jimmy's Apizza pull up in the driveway...

"Delivery...." He said as he got up to the door...

"That way..." she pointed as he, along with two other guys, brought in the following: Caesar salad, tossed salad, stuffed shells, chicken parmigiana, meatballs, sausage & peppers, chicken wings, and garlic bread with cheese...

"Thank you..." Keisha said as they placed everything on the counter and left.

"Yo – this a lot of food – who else comin'?" Troy asked...

"Well – beside you, Keisha, me, Bazil, and Beautiee – I also invited Sam, Joselyn, and Sheila..."

"Bazil won't be mad?" Keisha asked...

"Naa... Sam's his right hand man – and Beautiee loves his wife – and Sheila loves them all so..."

"I know that's right!" Keisha laughed...

"I can't believe Bazil though..." Troy said...

"Did you know Bazil got down like that?" Keisha asked...

"Nope..." Smalls answered...

"How'd you feel when you found out?" Troy asked...

"I was surprised – but not really…" Smalls answered…

"Watchu mean?"

"It is what it is…" Smalls said…

"I'on know if I could forgive Troy…" Keisha said…

"For real?" Troy asked…

"Babe – I love you to death – but I'on know if I could forgive all that – you fuckin' another man – then he tries to kill you – I don't blame Beautiee for shootin' his ass – I'da went ballistic too!" Keisha said…

"You don't blame Beautiee for shootin' who's ass?" Smalls asked…

"Both of them!" Keisha said…

"Keisha!" Troy yelled…

"Look – I love Bazil – y'all know that – but I told you when I met her I had a bad feeling…"

"Yea – you did – and I should 'a listened…" Troy said…

"Keisha – you had a bad feeling? About Beautiee?" Smalls asked…

"No – not about Beautiee…"

"About Bazil?"

"Smalls… I can't explain it… I just got a bad feeling…"

"Okay – let me ask you this – if you were on the jury…"

"Not Guilty!" Keisha interrupted…

"Oh okay – you had me worried…" Smalls said…

"She must really love him – she died and went to get him..." Troy said...

"I know! That's crazy!" Keisha said...

"When Bazil told me... he cried..." Smalls said...

"He did?" they both asked in unison...

"Yea..." Smalls said...

"Would you do that for me?" Troy asked Keisha as he pulled her into a kiss...

"We'd do it for each other..." Keisha said as she kissed Troy back...

"Ummmmm... y'all need a room?" Smalls laughed...

"Oh yea..." Troy said as he smiled...

"Hold on – somebody's at the door..." Smalls said as he went to get the door...

"Lovin' at first sight, lovin' me alright..." I sang...

"Yes... I love you..." Bazil breathed...

"Lovin' even when things ain't goin' right, Lovin' me all night 'till the mornin' light..."

"Love Me Baby..." Bazil sang with me...

"Lovin' me in spite of my many faults..." he sang as he touched my hair...

"Lovin' through the hurt, breakin' down my walls, Lovin' on my heart, kissin' all my scars..." I sang...

"Love Me Baby..." Bazil sang with me...

"Lovin' every day when I've lost my way..." he sang as we looked into each other's eyes... "Lovin' me is hard, don't know what to say..."

"Lovin' let's me know that you wanna stay..." I sang...

"Love Me Baby..." Bazil sang with me...

"Lovin' me in spite of it being hot..." he sang...

"Lovin' all the while even when I'm not..." I sang...

"Lovin' in the dark 'till you find the spot..."

"Love Me Baby..." we both sang...

"Lovin' how you touch, and I'm feelin' good..." I sang...

"Lovin' by my side like I knew you could..." he sang...

"Lovin' all along 'till I understood..." I sang...

"Love Me Baby..." we both sang...

"Hey!" Sam said as he grabbed Smalls into a hug...

"Hey Smalls..." Joselyn said as Smalls hugged her...

"They here yet?" Sheila asked as she came into the kitchen..."

"Well hello to you too..." Smalls laughed...

"I'm sorry – I just wanna get this up before they get here..." she said as she started pulling plates, napkins, cups, and banners out of a bag...

"Oh these are nice!" Keisha said... "Where'd you get these?"

"I ran out to the mall right quick..." Sheila answered as she opened everything...

"Aww... that's nice..." Troy said as he read the banner: 'Welcome Home.'

"They're gonna really like that..." Smalls said...

"Where are they anyway?" Sam asked...

"Don't rush them –le'me get these banners up and stuff..." Sheila said...

"Well they need to hurry up – 'cause I'm hungry..." Joselyn laughed...

"Aaight – le'me call 'em and see where they are..." Smalls said as he went into the library...

We melted into each other as Bazil pulled me closer, kissed me deeply, and we were making love again... until Bazil's cell phone rang...

"Yes Smalls..." Bazil answered without stopping...

"Yo – where the fuck are you?" Smalls asked...

"I'm... inside... Beautiee..." he breathed...

"I can't witchu – why'd you answer the phone?" he laughed...

"Because..." he breathed as I pulled him in deeper... "You wouldn't stop calling me... until I answered..."

"Hurry up... we're hungry..." Smalls laughed...

"Okay... we'll be there soon..." Bazil breathed as he dropped the phone on the floor...

"Is it time?" I breathed...

"Yes... it's time..."

"Okay..."

"We have to go..." he breathed and then he kissed me fully, covering my mouth with his while continuing to thrust deeper. I dug my fingers into the small of his back as my orgasm spread through my body and I started shaking. Bazil continued thrusting and came just as hard, kissing me so hard I nearly choked on his tongue...

"Hmmmmmph... Hmmmmmph... Hmmmmmpph..." I moaned, trying to catch my breath...

"Damn..." he breathed...

"I want more..."

"So do I..."

Chapter 5

"Uuuuggghhhhh! Mutha Fuckin' Toupe Wearin' No Dick Havin' Bastard!!!" Beverly yelled as she bust through the glass doors of the D.A.'s office...

"What the hell happened?" Detective Jones asked...

"We had her! We fuckin' had her!"

"They found her guilty?" Detective Jones said as she perked up...

"Yes!"

"Yesssss!!! I got 'em! First the husband – now the wife! I got 'em! Aaahhhhh..... Haaa..... Haaaa..... Haaa..... wait a minute... oh shit....."

"Exactly..."

"What the fuck happened?"

"Judge Duffey set the Guilty Verdict aside and entered a motion for acquittal..." Beverly answered as she fell down on the chair, holding her head in her hands, and sighed, shaking her head...

"What???"

"Yea..."

"How the fuck... Shit! Dammit!"

"He said – get this – he said the prosecution – me – failed to prove that Beautiee killed Trevor with malice or contempt..."

"Is he fuckin' blind? Can't he read? She said out her own mouth she slept with him to hurt her husband – Stevie Wonder could see motive! What the fuck is wrong with him?"

"He's sweet on her – that's what's wrong with him..."

No – no he's not... something else happened..."

"Detective... I saw it with my own eyes... she ran up to the bench and threw her arms around his neck... and he liked it..."

"I'm telling you – you're wrong about him... something else happened..."

"What makes you so sure?"

"I've known Judge Duffey for many years – he has a reputation – you heard how he was during the trial..."

"That was all an act – I'm telling you – she got to him... she got to them all...

"So... he fell for the tears... is that what you're saying?"

"The jury found her Not Guilty of the attempted murder of her husband..."

"I figured that would happen..."

"Really Detective?"

"C'mon Beverly – you know she didn't shoot him..."

"Okay... okay... but what about Sonia?"

"What about Sonia?"

"They found her Not Guilty of the murder of Sonia too..."

"Okay – wait – Not Guilty of her husband – Not Guilty of Sonia – but Guilty of Trevor?"

"Yea..."

"I knew it – I told you..."

"Told me what?"

"Let's just say Judge Duffey sentenced her..."

"As he should've..."

"Smalls would've filed an appeal... and he would've won..."

"Yea... you probably right..."

"He said she can't be Guilty of one and Not Guilty of the other two – right?"

"Damn – you really do know Judge Duffey..."

"Yes I do – but I also know something else happened..."

"You think so?"

"Trust me – I know Judge Duffey – something got to him – maybe she did tug on his heart – I saw her that night when they put her husband in the ambulance... it's possible she's not as bad as we think..."

"It's also possible we know exactly who she is... and she just got away with murder..."

"Wow! Really?"

"Trust me on this - I've been doing this job for a long time – my gut tells me she got away with murder..."

"What makes you so sure? She was pretty convincing on the stand... and when I went to speak to her..."

"Yea... she was nice... let you in... appeared to have nothing to hide... right?"

"Well... now that you mention it..."

"She played everyone... she slept with her husband's lover because she knew it would piss him off... she needed him to be angry at her... and he was... I wouldn't be a bit surprised if she didn't play Sonia too... she probably knew that Sonia would tell Trevor... Bazil has no idea who he married..."

"Damn Beverly – I never thought of it like that – who did he marry... really?"

"He married a Cunning, Manipulative, Condescending Bitch!"

"Beverly! I've never seen a case get to you like this!"

"She has our nemesis – Bazil Osgood – by his heart... and his balls... and she knows it... she saw him... she marked him... she was the damsel in distress... she needed to be rescued... and she needed him to rescue her..."

"Why him?"

"Why not him? He's the one man nobody can touch – he broke the law and went to prison and – even in prison – he managed to get the upper hand – we owed him – and we still owe him – and we can't get him – and now we can't get her... I thought Bazil met his match but in truth... Bazil's no match for her... She'll keep him as long as he lives... and when he dies... she'll move on with his money... his status... and she'll find someone else to rescue her..."

"Okay Beverly – I know you're mad 'cause you lost to Smalls – but you gotta get over it…"

"Mad? Oh no… I'm not mad about that – Smalls is a damn good attorney – I'm surprised at Judge Duffey though – I didn't think anyone could get to him – but Beautiee is the one that did…"

"I'm telling you – something else happened…"

"And I'm telling you – my gut is never wrong…"

"Bailiff…"

"Yes Your Honor?"

"Please have the court clerk send this flash drive overnight to the defendant and her husband asap…"

"Is that what I think it is?"

"That's exactly what it is…" Judge Duffey laughed…

"I can't believe you're actually doing this…" the Bailiff laughed…

"I wish I could be a fly on the wall to see Small's face when he gets it!" Judge Duffey laughed…

"Oh shit! You sent it to him too?"

"He's going to get an urgent email regarding his client with a video attached in 5… 4… 3… 2… 1!" Judge Duffey laughed as he hit send on his personal laptop…

"Oh shit! What if he files a complaint? What if he tries to have you removed from the bench?"

"He won't... trust me..."

"How can you be so sure?"

"I downloaded the 'sex tape' to that flash drive... erased it from the main server... and sent it to his personal email from my personal computer..."

"He may still try to file a formal complaint..."

"He might... but then he'd have to acknowledge that his clients were fucking in my court room... he'd have to defend them... and if he tried to impeach me, the entire committee would view his client's 'sex tape'... naaa... he won't do that..." Judge Duffey said as he smiled mischievously...

"Mmmmmm.... I don't wanna leave..." I breathed as we continued kissing...

"They're waiting... and they're hungry..."

"So am I..."

"I'll feed you again later..."

"Promise?"

"Promise..."

"Okay..." I sighed and got up out of bed...

"What's wrong?" Bazil asked as he watched me standing there shaking my head...

"I don't have anything to wear..."

"Check the closet..."

"Oh Bazil!" I cried when I saw the outfit from the night he proposed to me...

"Beautiee Osgood..." Bazil said as he got down on one knee and took my hand... "Will you marry me? Again?"

"Yes... my Thirst Quencher... yes..." I cried. Bazil took our wedding rings out the drawer to the end table and placed both rings on my finger. I took his ring, placed it on his finger, pulled Bazil's naked body close to me, and held him. "I love you so much my Thirst Quencher..." I said as tears streamed down my face...

"I love you too..." Bazil said as he pulled me into a kiss. "We better get dressed and get outta here..." he said as he dried my tears...

"Okay..." I sighed. We got dressed and started to leave when I stopped... "Bazil... wait a minute..."

"What's wrong?"

"Nothing..." I said as I picked up the prison jumpsuit off the floor...

"What are you doing with that?"

"I'm putting it where it belongs..." I answered as we left the room, closed the door, walked down the corridor, and I dropped it in the garbage can on our way to the lobby.

Chapter 6

"Surprise!" Everyone said as Bazil opened the door... and I burst into tears...

"Awww... Joselyn said as she started crying and hugged me..."

"I love y'all so much..." I cried...

"We love you too... stop crying..." Sam said as he fought back tears while hugging me...

"Stop crying man..." Bazil laughed as they hugged each other... "Thank you Joselyn..." Bazil said as he pulled Joselyn into a hug...

"What about me?" Sheila asked as she came over to us...

"What about you?" I laughed as we hugged each other...

"You don't need me to tell you how much I love you... but I'll tell you anyway... I love you..." Bazil said as he pulled her into a hug and kissed her on the cheek...

"Well... okay then..." Sheila blushed...

"Keisha..." I cried as we hugged each other...

"Stop cryin' – damn..." she laughed as she fought back tears...

"She's happy... and so am I..." Bazil said as he pulled Keisha into a hug...

"Bring it in man…" Troy said as he pulled Bazil away from his wife and hugged him…

"Smalls…" I breathed as I ran into his arms…"

"We did it!" Smalls said as he hugged me…

"You did it…" Bazil said as he hugged Smalls and I hugged Troy…

"Can we eat now? Please?" Joselyn laughed…

"Yes we can – we're just as hungry as you are…" Bazil laughed as we all went into the kitchen… and I started crying again…

"Damn – stop crying!" Keisha laughed as she started crying too…

"I can't help it… I'm so happy…" I cried as Bazil pulled me close to him…

"Hurry up and make them plates – maybe if we get some food in their mouths they'll concentrate on something else…" Smalls laughed…

"Awww shit!" Keisha and Troy said in unison as we all laughed. We all got plates… started eating… started drinking… and then there was another knock on the door…

"Bazil… somebody's at the door…" Smalls said as he started eating…

"It's for you…" Bazil said as we all continued eating…"

"Yo – aaight – you lucky I love you…" Smalls said as he got up to get the door…"

"Yo Bazil…" Troy laughed… "You funny…"

"It's for him…" Bazil said…

"How you know?" Troy asked...

"'Cause I do..." Bazil answered...

"Fina... Smalls said as he opened the door...

"Hey..." his wife, Josefina, said as she came inside...

"What are you doing here?" Smalls asked...

"Aren't you happy to see me?"

"Always..." Smalls said as he pulled her into a kiss...

"That's more like it..." she said as they continued kissing...

"C'mon... I'll introduce you..." Smalls said as he brought her into the kitchen... "Everyone... this is my love... my wife... Josefina..." Smalls beamed. I started tearing up as I remembered our conversation...

"Dammit Beautiee – why are you crying now?" Keisha laughed...

"I'm crying because I'm happy... dammit!" I laughed. I got up from the table and went over to Smalls and Josefina... "I'm Beautiee..." I said as I hugged her...

"It's nice to meet you..." she said as she hugged me back...

"Nice to see you Josefina..." Bazil said as he smiled and winked at her...

"Nice to see you too Bazil..." she said...

"This is Sam, his wife Joselyn, her mother Sheila, Keisha, and Troy..." I said as I acknowledged everyone at the table...

"Are you hungry?" Smalls asked...

"Yes I am..." she answered...

"Here..." Bazil said as he handed her a plate of everything...

"Something to drink?" Smalls asked...

"Maybe after I eat..." she answered...

"Can we talk?" Smalls asked...

"Sure..." she answered as she smiled. Smalls took her by the arm and they left the kitchen...

"I didn't even know Smalls was married..." Keisha said. "Me either..." Troy said.

"He doesn't really talk about his wife..." Bazil said...

"Why not?" Sheila asked...

"He likes to keep his private life private..." Bazil answered...

"C'mon – let's go dance this food and drink off..." I said. We all got up from the table and went into the living room...

"Please don't leave me Fina..." Smalls said as he closed the door to the library, took Josefina by the hand, led her to the couch, and sat her down beside him...

"I'm not leaving you..." she said as she ate her food...

"I thought you wanted a divorce?"

"I did..." she said as she continued eating...

"You did? Does that mean you changed your mind?"

"Yes my love – I've changed my mind..." she said as she put down her plate...

"Oh Fina..." Smalls breathed as he pulled her into a kiss... "I love you so much..."

"I love you too..." she said as he laid her down on the couch and they continued kissing...

"Where'd they go?" Sheila asked...

"They're in the library..." Bazil answered. Sheila, Joselyn, and Keisha ran to the floor to dance with me when Beyoncé's 'Love On Top' started playing. Bazil, Sam, and Troy laughed and fell on each other at our attempt to sing while doing the dance. It started out okay... but went left quickly...

"Nothing's Perfect!" Keisha laughed as she pushed in front of us, tripped, fell, and caused me to fall on top of her...

"Aaahhhh..... Haaa.... Haaa...." We all laughed...

"Damn girl – how much did you have to drink?" Keisha laughed...

"Not as much as you..." I laughed... "I get better when I'm drunk!" I laughed...

"C'mon ladies!" Bazil and Troy said as they both tried to help us up... and we pulled them down on the floor with us...

"What the hell kinda dancing is that?" Sam laughed...

"Line dancing – they all fell down – in a line!" Sheila laughed...

"Aaahhhh..... Haaa.... Haaa...." We all laughed...

"My love... we can't... not here..." Josefina breathed...

"Yes we can..." Smalls breathed...

"I don't want to get caught..."

"I'll lock the door..."

"What if he opens it?"

"He won't..."

"You sure..."

"Yes... I'm sure..."

"Okay..." she whispered. Smalls got up, locked the door, went back over to the couch, laid Josefina back down, and picked up where he left off...

"Dios te sientes tan bien... God you feel so good..." she whispered...

"Tú también... So do you..." he whispered as he unzipped his pants and continued kissing her. Josefina wrapped her arms around Smalls and pulled him down in between her legs as they continued kissing. Smalls was already excited but he got even more excited when he realized Josefina wasn't wearing anything underneath her skirt as he slid himself inside her. Josefina pulled him in deeper as she started whispering to him in Spanish...

"Sí mi amor ... hazme el amor ... te sientes tan bien dentro de mí... Yes my love... make love to me... you feel so good inside me..." Smalls loved it when she spoke Spanish – especially when they were making love... and he also knew he drove her crazy when he spoke to her in Spanish...

"Mi Fina ... te sientes tan bien conmigo ... te extrañé tanto ... te deseo ... Oh, sí ... My Fina... you feel so good to me... I missed you so much... I crave you... Oh yes..."

"Estoy corriendo ... Estoy corriendo ... I'm cumming... I'm cumming..."

"Estoy acabando contigo mi amor ... I'm cumming with you my love..."

"Sí ... ven conmigo ... oooohhhh ..... Yes... come with me... oooohhhh..."

"Uugghhh ... mierda ... uugghhh ... mierda ... uugghhh ... ¡mierda! ... Uugghhh... shit... uugghhh... shit... uugghhh... shit!" Smalls continued to lay with Josefina, kissing her tenderly for a few moments before he spoke...

"Vamos a casa... Let's go home..." he said as he got up and pulled her up into a kiss...

"OK, mi amor... Okay my love..." she said as they fixed themselves, unlocked the library door, and slipped out.

Chapter 7

We were so busy having fun we didn't see Smalls slip out with Josefina. "Oh shit – let's do this!" I said as I jumped up off the floor to dance to One Wine by Machel Montano & Sean Paul...

"I love the way she looks, pretty face and smile hold down on me..." Bazil and I started dry fucking but Keisha and Troy beat us to it. Sam and Joselyn were dancing like they danced on their wedding day but they were too busy looking at each other to notice anyone else, and Sheila had gone into the kitchen to get us more drinks... "And the way she move, in a di dance whining her body. It didn't take no time, I'm about to fall in love from one whine..." When Sheila came back into the living room with the drinks we were all whining and grinding so she sat down to finish her drink while she watched us...

"Now this is my music!" Sheila said as Where Do U Want Me to Put It started playing...

"Shit – this e'rbody's music!" Troy laughed as we all started dancing... "Time to get off..." Troy sang...

"Let's get it on..." Sam sang...

"Anytime you're in the mood to groove give me a call..." Bazil sang...

"Just say the word..." Troy sang...

"I'll be right there..." Sam sang...

"Baby I'm gonna fill you up with tender love and care..." Bazil sang...

"It's all to make you feel good... To carry you to ecstasy..." Troy sang as he pulled Keisha close to him and held her...

"If you gimmie directions, communicate to me..." Bazil sang as he pulled me close to him...

"Baby, tell me where do you want me to put it..."Sam sang as he pulled Joselyn close to him...

"Right here!" Joselyn and Sheila both said in unison as they both pointed between their legs...

"Aaaaa..... Haaaa..... Haaa.....!" we all laughed as we kept dancing...

"It's time to come closer... 'cause I've got the urge..." Troy sang to Keisha...

"So baby can we do it once or twice just to rehearse..." Sam sang to Joselyn...

"When can we work it out, when can we work it out now..." Sheila sang...

"Or do you like it when I get my groove on round and around and around and around..." Bazil sang to me...

"It's all to make us feel good in love even the blind can see, if we give you directions, just put it over here 'cause we told you where... where we want you to put it!" Keisha, Joselyn, and I sang...

"Put it right here – 'cause I'm tired..." Sheila said as she sat down..."

"Aaaaa..... Haaaa..... Haaa!" we all laughed as we kept dancing...

"Is it right here... is it over there... when we're makin' love..." Troy, Sam and Bazil sang...

"Y'all love to get us off!" Keisha, Joselyn, and I sang. We danced until the song was finished and then Sheila got up to leave...

"It's past my bed time – good night y'all..." she yawned...

"Yea... some of us have to work tomorrow..." Sam laughed...

"True... and my boss has a zero tolerance policy for lateness..." Joselyn laughed...

"I guess you better get going then... wouldn't want you to get in trouble with the boss..." Bazil laughed...

"Take some food – please..." I said.

"Can we take some drink too?" Sam asked...

"Sure..." I said as they went into the kitchen...

"Well... I guess we'll get going too..." Troy said...

"Guess again..." Bazil said...

"Ummmmm... okay... I guess we're staying Keisha..." Troy said as he sat back down...

"We're ready..." Sheila said as they came out of the kitchen...

"Thank you for everything – I love y'all..." I said as we took turns hugging each other...

"We love you too – see you soon..." Sheila said as she left and Joselyn and Sam followed.

"What's up Bazil?" Troy asked...

"You tell me..." Bazil said...

"Tell you what?"

"So... you have nothing you wanna ask me?"

"Oh... Yea..."

"Ask me..."

"Trevor?"

"What about him?"

"C'mon Keisha... let's let the men talk..." I said as I got up and she followed me into the kitchen...

"How long Bazil?"

"Doesn't matter..."

"That long?"

"Yea..."

"And you loved him?"

"Yes..."

"I thought you loved Beautiee?"

"I do..."

"How can you love Beautiee and Trevor?"

"I just do..."

"I don't understand it..."

"Neither do I..."

"So... you're gay?"

"No..."

"So how do you love a man... but you're not gay?"

"It's hard to explain..."

"Try...."

"Trevor was the only man I've ever been with..."

"So why do you think you're not gay?"

"I'm not gay because I don't want men – I don't desire men..."

"Only Trevor?"

"Only Trevor..."

"Wow – I couldn't do that to Keisha..."

"You're a better man than I am..."

"Don't say that Bazil... you're a good man... you just fucked up..."

"You don't have to tell me..."

"I'm sorry Bazil..."

"It's okay... you're right... I fucked up... and Beautiee still loves me..."

"You got a good one there – Keisha would'a been out!"

"You think so? She really loves you..."

"I'm tellin' you – Keisha would'a been out!"

"Beautiee blames herself..."

"Why? How is this her fault?"

"She asked me tonight how could I still love her..."

"Damn – she really feels this is her fault?"

"Yea..."

"Why?"

"Because she slept with Trevor..."

"Yo – when I heard her say that on the witness stand I was in shock…"

"I know…"

"I can't believe she did that – she was goin' through it…"

"She's still going through it…"

"She's home now – she'll be okay – she loves you after everything…"

"It's not going to be easy – I'll do everything I can to make it up to her – but she blames herself for everything…"

"Yo – you gotta tell her it's not her fault…"

"I do… every chance I get… but she still feels it's her fault…"

"Damn…"

"I asked her to run with me before they took her back to jail… and she said no…"

"What???"

"Yea…"

"Damn Bazil – God sent you a Queen…"

"He sure did… after everything I've done… God still came through for me…" Bazil said as he started tearing up…

"Don't start that shit Bazil…" Troy laughed…

"You still love me?"

"Yea Bazil… I still love you…"

"Good… I asked Beautiee to marry me again… and she said yes…"

"That's what's up…"

"I'm gonna do it right this time…"

"I know you will…"

"Let's put the food away and clean this up..." I said as I started to put the food away...

"Beautiee... wait a minute..."

"I'm okay Keisha..." I said as I went to put the baked ziti in the fridge... and dropped it... "Dammit!" I said as I started crying...

"You goin' be alright..." Keisha said as she hugged me...

"I messed up bad..." I cried...

"Wait a minute... how'd you mess up?"

"I slept with Trevor..."

"So did Bazil – it's crazy - but I understand it..."

"You do?"

"I'on know if I could'a done it if Troy cheated on me with a man – but if Troy cheated on me with a woman – I'd definitely cheat on him – that shit hurts – he'd need to know how it feels..."

"I hurt myself more than I hurt Bazil..."

"Really?"

"Yea... I never wanted him..."

"He wanted you though - if he didn't – he would'a told you no..."

"That's exactly what I said!" I laughed as we both cleaned up the baked ziti...

"Can I ask you a personal question?"

"It doesn't get more personal than this..." I laughed...

"Have you always liked women?"

"I never liked women..."

"Okay wait – I'm confused..."

"I always wanted to try a threesome with a woman and my husband – but I don't want to be with women..."

"Ohh... okay... so how did you wind up with Sonia?"

"Well... she was a shoulder to cry on..."

"Okay... I get that... so how'd you end up in bed with her?"

"We went out for drinks... she started telling me how she'd never been with a man because she saw how men treated her mother..."

"So she chose to be with women?"

"That's what she said..." I answered as we continued to put the food away...

"Hmmmmm... I don't get it..."

"I did it... and I don't get it either..."

"Did what?"

"I had sex with her... but I still love me some dick!" I laughed...

"Ohhh!" Keisha laughed...

"She tried to get me to leave Bazil for her..."

"Oh Shit! For real?"

"Yea... she kept telling me she couldn't understand how I could want Bazil after everything he put me through – she asked me if the dick was that good..." I didn't realize Bazil was standing there listening...

"What'd you tell her?"

"I told her – in a word – yes..." I laughed...

"She really wanted you to leave Bazil? For her?"

"Yea..."

"Damn Beautiee – you turned her out!" Keisha laughed...

"I didn't mean too – I never led her on – she knew I loved Bazil..."

"This shit's crazy!"

"It is! I wish I never invited her..." I said as I started to cry...

"C'mere girl – stop crying..."

"You don't understand – if I never invited her – none of this would'a happened!"

"You can't blame yourself Beautiee... you didn't know what would happen..."

"You don't understand..."

"What don't I understand Beautiee?"

"I didn't do any of it – she did!"

"Wait – what?"

"I invited her to come over – she told me the shit wasn't like the movies – she asked me if I was sure – I said yes..."

"Okay – so how is that you're fault – she said yes!"

"Because... she's the one that let Trevor in the house..." I whispered...

"Oooohhh!"

"I didn't realize it until Trevor dropped the gun when she got shot... he grabbed her, held her, and told me she wasn't supposed to die..." I cried...

"So – wait a minute – Sonia and Trevor set y'all up?"

"Yes! And it's all my fault!" I cried...

"Beautiee – it's fucked up – but it's not your fault – if anything – it's Bazil's damn fault!"

"That's what he says…"

"He does?"

"Yea…"

"Well he's right… I'on know if I would'a stayed with Troy after all that…"

"Really?"

"I love Troy to death… but I don't know if I could'a dealt with all that – and you went to jail too – Bazil needs to thank God for you…"

"He does… and I thank God for him too…"

"Really?"

"Yea… Bazil asked me to marry him again… and I said yes…"

"Damn – you really do love him…"

"Yes… I do…"

"He's a lucky man…"

"I'm the lucky one…"

Chapter 8

Bazil closed the door, picked me up and carried me upstairs without saying a word. Once we got upstairs he took me into the bedroom and tossed me on the bed...

"Come here my Thirst Quencher..." I said with open arms and spread legs. Bazil climbed on the bed slowly, crawled between my legs, laid down on top of me, and cried on my shoulder. I didn't say anything – I knew he needed to cry. He'd been strong for weeks – kissing my tears, reassuring me that everything was going to be okay – even when he wasn't sure of it – and now that everyone was gone – now that I was home – he could let it all out. I held him and let him cry as much as he needed to until he looked up at me and spoke...

"You promised me you'd never leave me..." he whispered through tear-soaked eyes...

"I'm sorry..." I whispered as I started to cry. He sat up on the bed and I sat up with him before he continued...

"I love you so much Beautiee... I'd give my life for you..."

"I know..."

"When I asked you to run with me... I needed you to say yes..." he said tearing up again...

"I wanted to Bazil..." I said as I cried...

"Then why didn't you?"

"I didn't want you to lose everything..."

"Beautiee..." he said as he pulled me into a kiss... "You're my everything..."

"Oh Bazil..." I cried...

"When I say I gotchu... please believe... I gotchu..."

"I know... I was scared Bazil..."

"Beautiee – you had nothing to be afraid of – I was ready – Smalls was ready..."

"Smalls?"

"Yes Beautiee..."

"I'm sorry... I didn't mean to hurt you..." I cried...

"I know baby... I know..." he said as he kissed me again...

"I didn't want to be on the run... I wanted to be free..."

"And you would have been..."

"How?"

"You would have been free – free from everything you went through in prison..." he whispered...

"It was so hard..." I whispered as I continued to cry...

"I know baby... I wanted to be there for you... I couldn't be there... I couldn't protect you... you could've died... and you would've gone through all that for nothing!" he said as he started crying again...

"Please don't cry Bazil... I'm sorry..." I cried...

"Beautiee... you have nothing to be sorry for... you were in there because of me...

"No Bazil..."

"Yes Beautiee... I'm the one that was with Trevor... I should've ended it with him as soon as I married you..."

"Bazil... I know you didn't mean to hurt me..."

"No I didn't... and I'll never hurt you again... I promise..." he cried as he kissed me again... "And I promise... they're going to regret the day they crossed me... and they'll regret the day they hurt you... every last one of them..."

"Bazil... please... it's over... I'm home... I missed you so much it hurt... let me make it up to you... please..." I whispered before I pushed him down on the bed, moved down between his legs, took his dick out his pants, and wrapped my mouth around it...

"Mmmmmm.... Yeesss... suck it..." he moaned as I sucked his dick slowly and deliberately. I moved up further on the bed and leveraged myself on his thighs, using my hands along with my mouth so I could take his dick in further... "Beautiee... Fuck..." he moaned as he grabbed my head with both his hands and fucked my mouth. I could feel his thighs tightening and

I relaxed my throat so I could take him in a little further... "I'm cummmmmiiinnnggg.... Ugggggghhhh!" I swallowed every drop, closed my eyes, and continued sucking softly while Bazil watched... "Mmmmmm... I missed this..." Bazil breathed as he played in my hair. I stopped sucking for a moment...

"I've dreamed of this moment so many times..." I said and then I went back to sucking...

"So have I..." Bazil breathed. I stopped sucking again...

"Did you... play with yourself while I was away?" I asked before I started sucking again...

"Mmmmmm...." He moaned... "No... I wanted to give it to you... Ooohhh.... Beautiee..."

"Mmmmmm... I'm... glad... you... waited... I was... starving..." I said between sucks...

"Come here Beautiee..." Bazil said as he pulled me up to his chest, took my face in his hands, and kissed me hard... "So..." he asked me between kisses... "Did you... play... with... yourself... while... you... were... away..."

"No... I wanted... you..."

"Did... your... pussy... ache..."

"Yeeess...."

"Did... your... pussy... throb..."

"Yyyeeessss...."

"Did... you... imagine... me... fucking... you?" he asked and then he turned me down on my back, opened my pants, and began playing with my pussy...

"Oh Bazil... yeeessss..." Bazil covered my mouth with his and tongued me hard as he pushed two fingers inside me and began finger-fucking me... "Mmmmmm.... MmmmMmmm.... MmmmMmmm..." I moaned in Bazil's mouth. Bazil increased his speed and I started coming all over his hand... "MmmmMmmm! MmmmMmmm! MmmmMmmm! MmmmMmmm! MmmmMmmm!" I moaned in Bazil's mouth as I came. Bazil took his hand out my pants, licked his fingers, and asked... "So... is that what you imagined..."

"Yessss... my Thirst Quencher..." I breathed...

"Let me show you what I imagined..." he said as he lifted me up, pulled off my shirt, removed my bra, laid me back down , and began kissing and sucking my breasts...

"Bazil..." I moaned as I pulled him down between my legs...

"Yes... Beautiee..." he answered as he removed my panties and my pants...

"Fuck me..." I breathed...

"Not yet..." he said as he kissed his way down my body... "I'm not done showing you what I imagined..." he said as he spread my legs and dove in...

"Baaazzziiillll!" I screamed as he began sucking my clit hard while simultaneously finger-fucking me...

"Yes... Beautiee..."

"Huuuu... Huuu... Huuu... Huuu... Huuu..." I moaned as I thrashed my head back and forth. "Mmmmmm... just like I imagined..." Bazil said and then went back to sucking my clit hard again... "Huuuu... Huuu... Huuu... Huuu... Huuu... Bazil...I'm cummmmmiiiinnnnggg!" I screamed as I arched my back and body up off the bed. Bazil continued to suck on my clit softly and finger-fuck me as my orgasm subsided until I spoke... "Bazil..." I panted...

"Yesss... Beautiee..." he answered while continuing to finger-fuck me...

"I'm a bit sensitive...

"Is that right?"

"Yesss..."

"Hmmmmm... let me see..." he said before starting to suck on my clit again...

"Huuu... Huuu... Bazil..."

"Hmmmmm... you are a bit sensitive... I'll give you a minute before I continue..." he said before getting up on his knees. Once he was up on his knees he removed his shirt, slid his pants and boxers off his ass, kicked them off his body, climbed up on top of me, and started kissing me...

"Mmmmmm..." I moaned... I missed you...

"I missed you too..." We continued kissing and holding each other for a few moments and then Bazil spoke... "Beautiee..."

"Yes... my Thirst Quencher..." I answered between kisses...

"Do... you... remember... what... I... told you?"

"When?"

"When... you... left... me... and... came... back..." he answered as he slid inside me and began fucking me...

"Yeeessss..."

"What... did... I... tell... you?"

"You... said... if... I... ever... left... you... again... oooohhh..."

"Go on..."

"You'd... fuck... me... to... death..."

"What... did... you... do?"

"I... didn't... mean... to... oooohhh..."

"I... know... but... you... did..."

"It... wasn't... my... fault..."

"Doesn't... matter... you... still... left... me... you... know... what... that... means..."

"Ohhhh... Bazil... Fuck me... Yeeesss..."

"So... tell me... what... does... that... mean?"

"It means... it means... Bazil... don't stop..."

"What... does... it... mean?" he growled as he started pounding my pussy..."

"It... means... I... I... have... to... pay... Aaaaagggghhhh!"

Chapter 9

"Oh Shit!" Smalls exclaimed when he opened his private email...

"Did I make your coffee too strong again?" Valarie, his paralegal assistant, asked...

"Uhh... no..."

"What's wrong then?"

"I need you to get Bazil on the phone – now!" he snapped...

"Good morning to you too..." she sighed as she left his office and went to get Bazil on the phone. Smalls was livid as he read his private email with the video attached:

Dear Smalls,

Attached you will find evidence that demonstrates your client's disrespectful behavior towards me and this court. As you are well aware, the Attorney General recently gained cabinet approval for a proposal to introduce the new offence of 'deliberately disrespecting the court'. This charge carries a penalty of 14 days in prison or fines up to $11,000 for each client; however, I do not intend to bring your clients up on additional charges for the following reasons:

1. Prior to observing your clients' behavior, I truly believe your clients have suffered enough. Although Mr. Osgood was annoying, to say the least, the only thing he was guilty of was wanting to be with his wife, and, being married myself, I can certainly understand that. As for Mrs. Osgood, I've never met any other defendant like her or had any other defendant like her in my court and now that I have, I'm a changed man – for the better. Often times when you get to the level where you're sitting on the bench, you're so busy handing down sentences that you forget that we all deserve compassion.

2. I watched the video, I enjoyed it, and I appreciate your clients (so did the Bailiff by the way – just so you know)... Haa... Haa...!

Just as you know I have no intention of bringing your clients up on charges or finning them, I hope I don't have to worry about you filing a complaint against me with the Judiciary Committee, trying to have me impeached, or trying to have me removed from this court.

Please know this evidence has been removed from the court server and has also been removed from the court's computer; however, before I did so, this evidence was downloaded to a flash drive and sent to your clients as a token of my appreciation.

Have a great day! Haa! Haa!

Cordially,

Judge Duffey

"MmmmMmmm...." I moaned as Bazil kissed me awake...

"Good morning..." he breathed as he started fondling my breasts...

"It certainly is..." I breathed...

"Still hungry?" he asked as he kissed my neck...

"Yeesss...." I moaned...

"Le'me feed you..." he breathed as he moved down in between my legs... and then his phone rang...

"Don't answer it..." I moaned...

"It's Smalls..." he said as he got up to answer his phone...

"Mutha fucka!" Smalls exclaimed as he pounded his fist on his desk and started the attached video. There was no sound but just as Smalls observed Bazil unzipping my prison jumpsuit he was interrupted via intercom...

"Mr. Smalls?" Valarie interrupted...

"Yes Valarie?"

"I have Bazil on the phone for you..."

"Thank you Valarie – oh – Valarie?"

"Yes Mr. Smalls?"

"I'm sorry about earlier..."

"Thank you Mr. Smalls..." Valarie said before she disconnected the intercom and connected Bazil...

"Good morning..." Bazil sighed happily...

"We need to talk..." Smalls said...

"I thought you and Josefina reconciled?"

"We did – but this isn't about her – it's about you... and Beautiee..."

"What's wrong?" Bazil asked as he put the phone on speaker so I could hear the conversation...

"Did you get a package from Judge Duffey?"

"Why – is he sending us a bill?" Bazil laughed...

"This isn't funny Bazil..." Smalls sighed...

"Damn Smalls... what's wrong?"

"I received an email from Juddge Duffey this morning... on my personal computer... with an attachment..."

"Okay – what's the problem?"

"Sigh... the problem is... he sent me a video..."

"A video?"

"Yes Bazil..."

"What are you trying not to tell me Smalls?"

"Is Beautiee there?"

"Good morning!" I said happily...

"He caught y'all on camera..." Smalls sighed...

"Oh shit!" Bazil exclaimed...

"Exactly..." Smalls said...

"Wait a minute – he sent you the video?" Bazil asked...

"Yea..."

"Did you watch it?" Bazil asked as I sat up in the bed...

"I was about to..." Smalls answered...

"Are we in trouble?" I asked...

"He said because the Attorney General gained cabinet approval for a proposal to introduce the new offense of 'deliberately disrespecting the court', you can each do 14 days in jail or be fined up to $11,000..." Smalls answered...

"Are you calling me to tell me we're going to jail Smalls?" Bazil asked...

"No..."

"Are you calling me to tell me we have to pay a fine totaling $22,000?"

"No..."

"So what are you calling to tell me?"

"He's not pressing charges or charging you with a fine because he thinks you've both suffered enough... but..."

"Smalls?" Bazil asked... "What's wrong?"

"He removed it from the server..."

"Okay – that's good – right?" I asked...

"Beautiee..."

"Yes Smalls?"

"He watched it... and so did the Bailiff..."

"Oh my God..." I sighed as I shook my head...

"I know what's on the video by your reaction..." Smalls said... "and I hate to tell you this... but I have to..."

"Oh God – what?" I asked...

"He sent you a copy..."

"What?!" Bazil yelled... "Oh shit – he didn't send us a bill – he sent us a sex tape!" Bazil laughed...

"Beautiee?"

"Yes Smalls?"

"You okay?"

"I guess so..." I sighed...

"I'm sorry..." Smalls said... "I'ma delete this shit right now – I just hope he didn't keep a copy..."

"Me too..." I sighed...

"So what if he did – fuck him!" Bazil laughed...

"I don't think it's funny...." I sighed...

"Beautiee?"

"Yes Bazil?"

"Are you sorry for what we did... or are you sorry we got caught?" he asked, smiling mischievously...

"I'm sorry we got caught... especially on camera..." I sighed...

"So..." he said as he put the phone down and pulled me close to him... "Knowing what you know now... if you could do it again... would you?" he asked as he started kissing me on my neck...

"Yeesss..." I moaned...

"Hello! I'm still on the phone!" Smalls laughed...

"Oh – sorry 'bout that – le'me call you back..." Bazil said as he hung up the phone, pulled me into a kiss, laid me down, and climbed on top of me.

Chapter 10

"Oh Damn!" Bazil exclaimed, waking me up...

"What's wrong?" I yawned...

"See for yourself..." he said as he turned the laptop towards me and I sat up...

"Oh Damn!" I laughed...

"Yea..." Bazil agreed...

"Welp... it's been confirmed... I suck a mean dick!" I laughed...

"Yes... yes... you do..." Bazil breathed as he pulled me into a kiss and then we both went back to watching...

"Oh my God – he has a camera in the ceiling!" I exclaimed...

"Indeed he does..." Bazil breathed as he started kissing me on my neck...

"Damn... you look as good as you made me feel..." I breathed as I watched him in between my legs, eating my pussy...

"Look..." Bazil laughed as he pointed to himself putting the handkerchief in my mouth...

"I couldn't help it..." I laughed as we continued watching... "Oh shit – I grabbed your head kinda hard – did I hurt you?"

"I didn't care..." Bazil breathed as he started kissing my neck again...

"Damn – you went in!" I exclaimed as I pointed to him fucking me with my legs in the air...

"Yes I did... just like you wanted me too..." he breathed as he pulled me into a kiss...

"I missed you..." I breathed in between kisses...

"I know..." he breathed...

"I was starving..."

"So was I..."

"Bazil... look..." I said as I stopped kissing to point at the laptop..."

"I love the look on your face when you cum..." he breathed as he pulled me back into a kiss...

"Oh Bazil... look..." I said as I pointed at the laptop and I started crying as we both watched me crying...

"I love you... Mrs. Osgood..." Bazil said as he pulled me into a kiss again...

"I love you too... my Thirst Quencher..." I breathed...

"Oh shit... look!" Bazil laughed as he pointed at the laptop...

"Damn!" I laughed... I was so busy trying not to get caught!" I laughed...

"Smalls said he was about to watch it..."

"I know..." I sighed...

"You think he watched it?"

"I know he did..." I answered...

"Well..." Bazil sighed... "Might as well put this flash drive away and read the enclosed letter..." he said as he removed the flash drive from the computer, put it in the night stand, took the letter out of the envelope and started reading:

Dear Mr. & Mrs. Osgood,

Enclosed you will find evidence that demonstrates your disrespectful behavior towards me and this court. The Attorney General recently gained cabinet approval for a proposal to introduce the new offence of 'deliberately disrespecting the court'. This charge carries a penalty of 14 days in prison or fines up to $11,000 for each of you; however, I do not intend to bring either of you up on additional charges for the following reasons:

1. Prior to observing your behavior, I truly believe you have suffered enough. Although Mr. Osgood was annoying, to say the least, the only thing he was guilty of was wanting to be with his wife, and, being married myself, I can certainly understand that. As for Mrs. Osgood, I've never met any other defendant like you or had any other defendant like you in my court and now that I have, I'm a changed man – for the better. Often times when you get to the level where you're sitting on the bench, you're so busy handing down sentences that you forget that we all deserve compassion.

2. I watched the video, I enjoyed it, and I appreciate you (so did the Bailiff by the way – just so you know)... Haa... Haa...!

Just as you know I have no intention of bringing you up on charges or finning you, I hope I don't have to worry about you filing a complaint against me with the Judiciary Committee, trying to have me impeached, or trying to have me removed from this court.

Please know this evidence has been removed from the court server and has also been removed from the court's computer; however, before I did so, this evidence was downloaded to a flash drive before I send it to you as a token of my appreciation.

Have a great day! Haa! Haa!

Cordially,

Judge Duffey

"Well..." Bazil sighed... "What are we going to do?"

"Nothing..." I sighed...

"Nothing?"

"What can we do? We've done enough already..." I sighed...

'"He shouldn't get away with this..."

"Neither should we... but we did..."

"You have a point."

Chapter 11

"I'm ready to go back to work... at your company... and mine..."

"Why do you want to keep your LLC?"

"Because I do..."

"Well – Smalls can help us set it up where your LLC is underneath my corporation – this way we have one company together, protect our assets, streamline the business bookkeeping, and simplify our marketing."

"I like that..."

"You do?"

"Yes..."

"Hmmm... I thought you'd object..."

"Why?"

"Well... I thought you might want to continue to be a Sole Proprietor..."

"I'm going to continue to be a Sole Proprietor... under my husband..." I said as I moved closer to Bazil...

"Mmmmm... under your husband... I like that..." he breathed before pulling me into a kiss...

"So do I..." I breathed as I kissed him back...

"Are you hungry?"

"Always..." I breathed as he laid me down on the bed and climbed on top of me...

"Let me feed you then..." Bazil said before kissing me fully...

"Bazil..."

"Yesss... Beautiee..." he said in between kisses...

"We... need... to... talk..."

"Okay..." he sighed disappointedly... "What's wrong?" he asked as he rolled off of me, lay down beside me, and propped himself up on his elbow...

"Nothing..." I sighed as I turned to face him..."

"Beautiee..." he said as he stroked my hair... "Talk to me..."

"I want to tell my story..."

"Wait a minute..."

"I want to tell my story..."

"You mean... about us?"

"Yes..."

"Hmmmmm... I don't know..."

"My readers already know what happened to me... and so does everybody else..."

"I was hoping we could put it behind us..." Bazil sighed...

"Okay... never mind..." I sighed as I went to get up but Bazil pulled me back down onto the bed...

"Beautiee... wait..."

"Forget it... I won't do it..."

"You can do it..."

"Really?"

"Yes..."

"It's going to be very personal..."

"I know..."

"And you're okay with that?"

"Not really..."

"Then I won't do it..."

"You have to do it..."

"I don't understand... I thought you didn't want me to do it?"

"I don't want you to... but I know you need to..."

"I still don't understand..."

"You've been through a lot... you have a story to tell..."

"Yes I do..."

"And you want to tell your story..."

"Okay..."

"And I'm a big part of your story..."

"Yes you are..."

"Maybe that's a good thing..."

"It is... it is..." I said as I pulled him into a kiss..."

"So... have you started working on your story yet?"

"I started working on my story when I was in jail..."

"You did?"

"Yea..."

"How'd you find the time?"

"Once I started writing, I couldn't stop – I wrote the song, and then I started writing my story..."

"Where'd you get the pen and paper?"

"Deputy Warden Hein gave it to me... he said it would keep me outta trouble while I was in there..."

"Hmmmmm... that was nice of him... I'll have to thank him..."

"I already tried to thank him – and he refused..."

"He refused?"

"Yea – after he gave me the pad he let me talk to you..."

"Yes... I remember..."

"So I tried to give him a hug and he refused..."

"Yea – Nathan's like that – keeps him from being brought up on charges of sexual harassment..."

"Oh right – I didn't think of that..."

"So can I read what you've written so far?"

"You promise not to critique it?"

"What'da you mean?"

"I mean don't be my publisher – don't be my editor – don't correct my grammar – don't change my words – don't make suggestions – just read it!" I snapped...

"Okay Beautiee..." he laughed... "I promise..."

"Okay... here..." I said as I pulled my pad out, handed it to Bazil, and he started reading:

Chapter One

I was completely done. I was psychologically, emotionally, and physically drained. I knew I shouldn't be turning to alcohol, but it was either a drink or a shotgun and since I couldn't get my hands on a shotgun, a drink would have to do. I sat there admiring the glass of amaretto sour in front of me, picked up the cherry, and slid it into my mouth. I closed my eyes, tilted my head back slightly, and imagined the liquor going down my throat, quenching my thirst, and numbing the pain I was in. I opened my eyes and as I reached for the glass, he wrapped his hand around my hand and held the drink with me. "Who are you?" I asked as I watched him pick up the glass and take a sip with both our hands holding it...

"I'm your Thirst Quencher," he answered as we put the glass down, he leaned towards me, and began kissing me slowly and softly, sliding his tongue in my mouth, allowing me to suck the amaretto flavor. I couldn't take my eyes off of him. It was hot inside and out, and I admired the sweat dripping from his chocolate temples. We picked up the glass again and he took another sip, but this time when he leaned in to kiss me he used his tongue to pour the amaretto into my mouth, sliding his tongue in a little deeper, allowing me to suck and swallow. We lifted the glass again and before he could take a sip, I brought the glass to my mouth and gulped the rest of the drink down. He looked at me with such a sad face and turned to leave but before he could, I turned him back towards me, took his face in my hands, and kissed him fully in the mouth, sliding my tongue into his so he could suck the amaretto flavor. We pulled away from kissing and I was relieved to see I changed his mind.

"Who are you?" he asked.

"I'm Beautiee," I answered as I lowered my head.

"Look at me," he whispered as he gently placed his hand under my chin and picked my head up. "What happened?"

"Long story," I answered as I tried to lower my head but couldn't. When I tried to turn my head away from him, he wouldn't allow it.

"Look at me," he whispered as he turned my head to face him. "I've got all night," he said as he looked into my face.

"I don't want to..."

"It's okay... you don't have to," he said as he stood up. "Come with me... please..." he whispered as he held out his hand. I stood up, took his hand, and allowed him to lead me to the elevator. I knew where we were going but I didn't care... I needed to numb the pain I was in and I was going to numb it one way or the other. The way I figured, this way was better than a shotgun. When the elevator doors opened, I realized where I was and started having second thoughts...

"I can't do this," I whispered as I backed up into the elevator. He stood in the door, blocking it from closing...

"Don't leave me Beautiee... please..." he whispered as he extended his hand for me to take. I took his hand again and allowed him to lead me out the elevator down the hall and into his room. Once inside, I looked around the suite, admiring the décor. The master bath was off to the right with two sinks, porcelain countertops, recessed lighting, and marble floors, and a shower build for two. The king size bed was to the left, made up with brown, cream, and red comforters and pillows. In the middle of the room was a chocolate chaise lounge, and to the right of that was a desk with a computer, a lamp, paper, pens, and a phone. "Make yourself comfortable," he said as he sat down on his bed and patted, motioning for me to sit down next to him.

"I'd like to take a shower," I said as I opened the closet door and took the robe off the hanger.

"Whatever you want," he said, looking at me seductively.

"I need another drink" I said as I walked over to the chaise lounge and sat down.

"Amaretto sour?" he asked.

"I need something a little stronger... something to take the edge off..."

"I'll make you another amaretto," he said, completely ignoring my request. When he sat down on the chaise lounge next to me with the drink, I reached for the drink but he playfully pulled it away, smiling. "Say please," he commanded.

"Please," I said sarcastically.

"You can do better than that," he replied just as sarcastically.

"Look," I said as I turned to face him.

"Yes Beautiee?" he said as he turned to look at me. I could tell he was really enjoying this...

"Who are you?" I asked.

"I'm your Thirst Quencher," he answered, still holding the drink...

"The ice is beginning to melt... and I'm really thirsty..."

"Here," he said as he handed me the glass and I wrapped my hand around his hand.

"Thank you," I replied, slowly taking a sip and pulling the glass away. He watched me swallow and as we both dropped the glass, he pushed me back onto the chaise lounge and began kissing me forcefully. He slowed down when he sensed I wasn't enjoying it and continued kissing me softly and sensually, sucking my tongue, tasting the amaretto. "MmmmMmmm..." he moaned between kisses, moving from my mouth to my neck...

"Don't..." I whispered...

"Please..." he panted while continuing to kiss my neck...

"I... need..." I tried to explain between kisses...

"You... need... to... let... me... be... your... Thirst... Quencher...

"Shower..." I panted...

"Okay... I'll join you..." I didn't want him to...

"No..." I panted...

"Please..."

"I'll be right back..."

"I'm... coming... with... you..."

"Okay..." I relented.

"Come with me," he said as he stood up and reached for my hand. I took his hand, stood up, picked up the robe, and let him lead me to the shower. I stepped into the bathroom and watched him come up behind me in the mirror. He unzipped my dress and began kissing my neck as he slid my dress off my shoulders and it fell to the floor. He was pleasantly surprised when he saw I was naked underneath. He quickly disrobed, dropping his clothes to the floor, turning me around to face him. His look quickly changed from seductive to hurt when he saw the bruises on my body. I tried to look away but he placed his hand under my chin, turned me to him, pulled me close to him, and kissed me. He reached to turn on the shower, took me by the hand, and let me inside. I stood underneath the water and let it soothe me as he reached for the *shampoo, squirting some in his hands. He began to massage my scalp while simultaneously kissing the back of my neck.*

"Mmmmmm..... that's nice..." I moaned as I began to relax...

"Ouch... what the... oh my God... Beautiee..." he whispered as he pulled his left hand away to look at the blood. I couldn't turn to look at him. I just continued to stand under the water, facing the wall, until he turned me around to face him... "Beautiee... this is glass... I need to check to see if you're still bleeding... you might need stitches... let me rinse this out... I'll try not to hurt you... be still..." he said as the shampoo ran down my head and face... "Turn your head this way... it looks like you might need stitches...

"No... I said, shaking my head.

"Let's get you cleaned up," he said completely ignoring me, until... "What are you doing?"

"What does it feel like I'm doing?" I asked him as I continued 'washing' his dick.

"It... feels... nice..." he moaned as I continued soaping him up and down. I loved watching the creamy lather run down his chocolate body.

"Ouch," I said as he started soaping my bruises.

"I'm sorry Beautiee," he whispered as he pulled me into a passionate kiss. I could feel his erection against me and I wanted him – needed him. I felt safe and secure in his arms and I

wanted to stay in them for as long as I could. We stopped kissing and I wrapped my arms around him as he continued to hold me against him. "Come here," he whispered as he led me out the shower towards the bench. I sat down and he gently towel-dried my hair, being particularly careful on the left side of my head. "It looks like the bleeding stopped... you may not need stitches," he said as he continued to dry me off and then himself. When he was finished he lifted me up off the bench, careful not to grab me by my bruises, carried me to the bed, and gently laid me down on the bed. He lay behind me and pulled me close to him, spooning me, kissing me softly on my neck and shoulder.

"You... feel... so... good...," I yawned as I drifted off the sleep...

Bazil didn't say anything. He put the pad down on the night stand and looked at me with tears in his eyes. He pulled me close to him, kissed me, and held me as he cried for a few moments and then he spoke... "Oh my God... Beautiee... I love you so much..."

"I love you too... my Thirst Quencher..."

"I know... I can't believe it... the way you wrote about me... you made me seem so gentle... so loving..."

"You are gentle... you are loving..."

"I saw you... and I knew..."

"I knew too..."

"Were you really thinking about killing yourself?"

"I was in pain... and I was on a mission to numb it as best I could... and the bar was right there..."

"And so was I..."

"And you're still here..."

"Damn right I am..." he said as he pulled me into a kiss...

"So you like my story so far?"

"I love it..."

"It's going to get worse..."

"I know..."

"You're still okay with it?"

"Yesss..."

"Good..."

"So... are you going to leave anything out of your story?" Bazil asked as he started kissing me on my neck..."

"I'm an erotic fiction publisher..." I moaned... "My readers expect erotica..."

"Mmmmmm...." He moaned as he kissed me... I can't wait to read it..."

"I can't wait to write it..." I moaned as he lay me down on the bed..."

"Will I get to read more?" he asked as he climbed on top of me, spread my legs, slid himself inside me, and started thrusting...

"Yeesss..." I moaned.

Chapter 12

"What time is it?" I yawned...

"It's a little after 12..." Bazil answered as he bent down to kiss me...

"Mmmm... why didn't you wake me up?"

"It's been so long since I've seen you sleeping peacefully..."

"I missed this bed..." I sighed...

"Is that all you missed?' he asked, looking at me mischievously...

"I missed you..."

"Oh yea?"

"Bazil!"

"I missed you too..." he said as he bent down to kiss me again...

"I missed waking up, having morning sex, and going to work with you..." I said as I sat up...

"I missed that too..." he said as he took off his robe, pulled back the covers, and got back in bed with me...

"Did you work while I was away?"

"I tried... but I couldn't..."

"That was the worst thing I've ever been through in my life..."

"I know... I'm sorry..."

"I'm glad they're dead..."

"Beautiee..."

"I'm serious..."

"I know…"

"They wanted us dead… and for what?" I said as I started crying…

"Beautiee… no… please don't cry…" he said as he kissed me…

"Let's get married…"

"Okay…"

"Let's renew our vows in the courthouse…"

"Okay…"

"Ooohhh… I have an idea…"

"What?"

"Let's ask Judge Duffey to marry us again… in his old chambers!" I laughed…

"I love it!"

"You do?"

"Beautiee…" he breathed as he kissed me… "I… love… anything… that… makes… you… happy…"

"Okay!" I squealed as he kissed my neck and nibbled on my earlobe…

"So… how big do you want it?" I bust out laughing…

"What's so funny?"

"You just asked me how big do I want it!" I laughed…

"Oh shit!" he laughed… "That big huh?" he laughed again…

"Yea…" I laughed…

"You really want a big wedding?"

"How many people did we have in this house welcoming me home?"

"A lot…" he sighed…

"I want all of them at our wedding..."

"Okay..."

"I can wear my dress again..."

"I can wear my tux again..."

"When should we do it?"

"We can do it whenever you want..." he breathed as he kissed me...

"Let's go downstairs..."

"I need pussy..." he breathed as he pulled me down in the bed and climbed on top of me...

"So..." I laughed...

"So? What's that supposed to mean?" he snapped as he jumped up off me...

"It means..." I said as I got up out the bed, went over to him, put my arms around his neck, and kissed him... "You don't have to be upstairs..." I said as I kissed him again... "To get pussy..."

"Ohhh... that's right... now I remember..." he breathed as we continued kissing...

"You can get... pussy... in the living room..."

"I can get pussy... in the kitchen..."

"I have an idea..."

"Tell me..."

"Let's celebrate... by fucking... in the pool..."

"We can do that..."

"I need coffee first..."

"Me too..."

"And I need to eat..."

"Me too..."

"And I can suck your dick under water..."

"Okay – that's it – let's go!" Bazil said as he grabbed me by the hand...

"Wait – le'me get a robe..." I laughed. Bazil waited for me to get a robe and we went downstairs.

Chapter 13

"C'mon..." Bazil said as he pulled me into the kitchen...

"Can I sit down now?" I laughed...

"No..." he breathed as he pulled me into a kiss...

"Mmmm... okay..." I sighed...

"I'm gonna make us some coffee..."

"Okay..." I laughed as I sat down at the table...

"Get up..."

"Huh?"

"Get up." I did as I was told...

"Yes my Thirst Quencher?"

"Come here." I went over to where Bazil was standing and he pulled me close to him...

"I'm gonna make us some coffee..." he breathed as he started kissing me on my neck...

"Okay..." I laughed...

"Am I tickling you?"

"A little..." I laughed again...

"Stay here..." he said as he went back to making coffee. Bazil looked at me a few times, smiling mischievously, as he made coffee. When the coffee was ready, he added hazelnut creamer, added sugar, put the coffee on the table, and then he sat in the chair... "Do you remember what you said to me at the hotel?"

"Yes my Thirst Quencher!" I squealed as I hurried over to him, opened my robe, and sat on his dick...

"Now..." he said as he picked up his cup and took a sip... "I want you to take your time... so you don't burn yourself..."

"Okay..." I moaned as I started riding his dick slowly and picked up my coffee...

"Mmmm..." I moaned as I sipped it...

"Good.. isn't it?"

"Yeesss..." I moaned as I started riding his dick a little faster...

"Slow down... I don't want you to spill your coffee..." Bazil smiled at me mischievously as he sipped his coffee. He knew that he was torturing me and he was enjoying it...

"There..." I breathed... "I'm finished..." I breathed again as I put the cup down on the table, put my arms around his neck, and started riding his dick faster...

"Uh uh... slow down... I'm still drinking my coffee..." I slowed down, but I didn't stop...

"You want me to fuck you... don't you?"

"Yes... my Thirst Quencher..." I moaned as I continued riding his dick...

"Okay... I'm done..." he breathed as he put his cup down on the table, grabbed my ass with both hands, pushed me down on his dick, and started fucking me...

"Bazil! Haah... Haah... Haah..."

"Yesss... Beautiee... Uuugh! Uuugh! Uuugh! Uuugh!"

"Fuck me! I'm cumming! Aaaaahhhh!"

"Uuugh! Uuugh! Uuugh! Uuugh! Uuuugggghhhhh!"

"Oh my God..." I breathed as I pulled him into a kiss and kissed him hard...

"Mmmm.... Did you... enjoy... your... coffee?"

"Yes my Thirst Quencher... yes..."

"Mmmm... good... now... I'll make us breakfast..."

"Mmmm... okay..."

"You want more... don't you?"

"Yes... my Thirst Quencher..."

"I'll make us breakfast..."

"Mmmm Hmmmm..."

"We'll eat breakfast..."

"Mmmm Hmmm..."

"Then we'll go out to the pool..."

"Mmmm Hmmm..."

"Then I'll give you more..."

"Okay..." I breathed as I got up off his lap and sat in the chair...

"What would you like to eat?"

"Scrambled eggs, bacon, and French toast..." I sighed...

"Coming right up..." he said as he went over to the refrigerator, took out everything he needed, and started cooking...

"Damn that smells good..." I sighed. Bazil didn't respond – he just continued cooking until everything was ready. I smiled at him mischievously as he put the plates on the table...

"When do you want to go back to work?" he asked as we started eating...

"I wanna try to go back on Monday..."

"Try?"

"Yea..."

"Beautiee?"

"Yes Bazil?"

"What's wrong?"

"Part of me wants to go back to work... but..."

"You don't think you can face them – right?"

"Yea..."

"They were in court with us..."

"I'm not talking about them..."

"Who are you talking about then?"

"Everybody else..." I sighed... "I went in on my first day – I took charge – fired MaryJane – promoted Joselyn – and now..." I said as I teared up... "I'm a fuckin' mess..."

"Beautiee..." Bazil said as he got up, pulled me up out the chair, and held me... "You're not a mess... you're beautiful..." he said as he kissed me... "and you're strong..."

"I just feel like I messed up everything..." I sighed...

"I'm going to tell you this one more time..." he said as he kissed me... "and I need you to understand me... okay?"

"Okay..."

"None of this was your fault..."

"But Bazil..." Bazil pulled me into a kiss and kissed me hard to keep me from talking... "I see I have my work cut out for me..." he sighed...

"I like that..."

"What?"

"I like how you kiss me when you want me to be quiet..." I laughed...

"There you are..." he said as he smiled...

"You ready to go swimming?"

"Oh yea..." he answered as he took me by the hand and led me outside...

"Can anyone see us?" I asked as I dropped my robe...

"No... all the windows face the street or the bedroom directly across from their houses..." Bazil answered as he took off his robe... "The windows in the back of the houses face their backyards – it's completely private..." he said as I went over to the diving board, walked up the stairs, walked down to the edge, and jumped in...

"Oooohhhh... it's cold... but it's nice..." I said as I came up out the water...

"Wait for me..." Bazil said as he climbed up the steps, walked out to the edge, and jumped in... "You're right... it's cold..." he laughed as he swam over to me and took me in his arms...

"I love you..."

"I love you too..." he said as he pulled me over to the side of the pool...

"This is nice..." I sighed...

"It is nice..." he breathed as we started kissing...

"Troy!"

"Yea Keisha?"

"Bazil got a package delivered..."

"Okay..."

"Troy!"

"Aiigght..." he laughed... "I'm coming..."

"It's from Vegas..."

"Oh shit – I bet it's their wedding pictures! You gonna open it?"

"Hell no – I'm gonna go inside and make them open it..." Keisha said as she unlocked the door and they came inside...

"Bazil... Haah... Yes..."

"You like that?"

"Yes... Just like that..."

"Cum for me..."

"Ooohhh... Ooohhh... Ooohhh... I'm cumming... Yes... I'm cumming... Aaaagh!"

"Was it good?"

"Hell yea..."

"Good... you ready?"

"I'm ready..." I breathed as I lowered myself under the water and took Bazil's dick in my mouth...

"Bazil? Beautiee?" we got a package for y'all..." Keisha called out...

"Damn – it smells good in here..." Troy said as they went into the kitchen...

"Beautiee... shit... why'd you stop?"

"I can only hold my breath for about 20 seconds..." I breathed as I went back under the water and took his dick in my mouth again...

"They're here — look — they left plates on the table... Bazil? Beautiee! Where y'all at?" Keisha yelled...

"Let's go upstairs..." Troy said as Keisha followed him upstairs...

"Damn..."

"I'm sorry..." I breathed...

"Don't be..."

"Okay..." I breathed as I went back under the water and took his dick back in my mouth. Bazil grabbed my head with his hands and started fucking my mouth harder so I knew he was close to cumming...

"Shit — where the fuck are they?" Keisha asked as she stood at the top of the steps...

"Maybe they're in the pool..." Troy said as he went downstairs and Keisha followed...

"Beautiee... Fuck... I'm Cumming... Uuuugggghhhh!"

"Hey Bazil..." Keisha panted... "We was lookin' all over for y'all — you got a package — where's Beautiee?"

"Right here!" I breathed as I came up from under the water as Bazil and I held each other...

"Oh damn – yo – I'm sorry – c'mon Keisha..." Troy said as he turned to leave...

"Wait!" I yelled...

"Yea?" Keisha asked...

"Pass us our robes..." I laughed...

"Troy – pass me them robes..."

"Here..." Troy said as he picked up the robes, closed his eyes, and turned his back...

"Troy - open your eyes – you ain't gonna see shit..." Keisha laughed...

"Aiight here – take these robes – I'ma go sit in the living room..." he said as he handed Keisha the robes...

"Aiight – I'll see you in a minute..." she told Troy... "I'ma put your robes here so you can get out – I'll see y'all in the living room..." she told us before she went inside...

"Damn I love you..." Bazil said as he kissed me...

"Mmmm... that good?"

"Hell yea!"

"I can't wait for you to do me in the water – when I start cumming I'ma lock my legs around your head and suffocate you..."

"Beautiee..." Bazil breathed as he kissed me...

"Yes... my Thirst Quencher?"

"I can hold my breath longer than you can..." he breathed as he kissed me again...

"I knew we shouldn't a came over here – we should 'a just took the package home..." Troy said...

"Calm down Troy – it's not that serious..." Keisha laughed...

"Keisha! We caught her suckin' his dick!"

"No we didn't!"

"What was she doing under the water then?"

"She was suckin' his dick!" Keisha laughed...

"See?"

"No Troy – we might know what she was doin' – she might tell us what she was doin' – but we didn't actually see her doin' it..."

"You right..."

"Troy?"

"Yea?"

"You want me to do that?"

"Oh shit – you serious? I'm wit it!"

"I suck ya dick in the bedroom, I suck ya dick in the shower, I suck ya dick in the pool – what's the difference?"

"How long can you hold your breath under water?"

"I'on know – 10-15 seconds maybe..."

"Oh shit – I'm ready – let's go..."

"Leaving so soon?" Bazil laughed as we came into the living room...

"I'm sorry..." Troy said...

"Don't be – it's cool..." Bazil said...

"See Troy? They aiight..." Keisha said...

"It must be urgent..." I said...

"What?"

"You said you were looking all over the house for us..."

"Oh yea – y'all got a package..."

"Bazil?"

"Yes Beautiee?"

"Didn't I ask you if anybody else had a key to the house?"

"Yes Beautiee..."

"What did you say?"

"I said nobody else has a key..." Bazil sighed...

"Damn Beautiee – I'm sorry..." Keisha said...

"I'm not talking to you Keisha – shut up – and give me the package..." I laughed...

"Here..." she said as she handed me the package...

"Ooohhh! Our wedding!" I squealed as I started jumping up and down...

"Can we see it?" Keisha asked...

"Okay!" I squealed...

"C'mon Bazil – let's go get dressed – Keisha – Troy – go get a bottle of champagne – and four glasses!" I squealed as I took Bazil by the hand and pulled him towards the stairs...

"Mrs. Osgood?"

"Yes Mr. Osgood?"

"C'mere..." he said as he picked me up in his arms and carried me upstairs...

"You sure know how to spoil me..." I sighed...

"This is only the beginning..." he said as he put me down and pulled me into a kiss...

"Bazil... we have company..."

"They can wait..." he whispered as he took me by the hand, pulled me into the bathroom, turned the shower on, and led me into the shower...

"Bazil... We..." Bazil kissed me hard and held me as the water beat down on us. I couldn't move if I wanted to... and I didn't want to. I wrapped my arms around his neck and my legs around his waist as he eased himself inside me... "Hmmph... Hmmph... Hmmph... Hmmph..."

"Mmmph! Mmmph! Mmmph! Mmmph! Mmmph!"

"Hmmph... Hmmph... Hmmph... Hmmph.... Hmmph..."

"Mmmph! Mmmph! Mmmph! Mmmph! Mmmph!"

"HMMPH! HMMPH! HMMPH! HMMPH! HMMPH!"

"MMMPH! MMMPH! MMMPH! MMMPH! MMMPH!"

"That's it – I'm gonna have my coffee in the morning – we're gonna fuck in the pool – then we're gonna fuck in the shower!" I panted...

"We can do that..."

"Let's hurry up and get outta here and get dressed..." I breathed...

"Okay..." he breathed as he took the shampoo and started washing my hair...

"It's gonna take a while to dry..."

"Don't worry about that..." he said as he finished washing my hair... "Close your eyes – I'm gonna rinse your hair..." I closed my eyes as Bazil rinsed my hair... and then... "What are you doing?"

"What's it feel like I'm doing?" I asked as I washed his dick with my hands...

"I'm going to make you pay for this later..." he whispered in my ear...

"I'm looking forward to it..." I whispered back as we got out the shower, dried off, got dressed, and went downstairs...

"We made sandwiches..." Keisha said as she ate... "Hope y'all don't mind..."

"Did you make us one?" Bazil asked...

"Yea..." Troy laughed...

"Then we don't mind..." Bazil laughed...

"Oooohhh... look at our pictures!" I squealed as we put them on the table...

"Damn Bazil – you look good – don't he Troy?" Keisha asked as she passed some of the pictures over to Troy...

"Yea... he looks good..." Troy answered as he smiled...

"Thank you..." Bazil said...

"Oh my God! Beautiee!" Keisha whispered as she started crying...

"Don't start Keisha!" I laughed as we hugged...

"You look so beautiful..."

"Thank you..." I said as we hugged each other, crying...

"You should send Smalls a couple of these..." Troy said...

"You should let us get a couple of pictures..." Keisha said...

"We'll go through them – and you'll get a couple..." Bazil said...

"You should let us take a couple now..." Keisha said...

"Keisha – wait a minute..." Troy laughed...

"Why I gotta wait a minute? Don't y'all love me? Ain't I special?"

"Of course you are..." Bazil said as he pulled Keisha into a hug and kissed her on her cheek...

"See Troy – I'm special..." Keisha gushed...

"You can have one picture..." Bazil said...

"Can Troy have one too?"

"Yea..." I sighed...

"I love y'all!" Keisha squealed...

"C'mon Troy – let's pick..."

"I want one of each!" Troy laughed...

"How 'bout this?" Bazil asked as he picked up the photos and put them back in the envelope... "I'll make you a complete set..."

"You will?"

"Yes Keisha – but there's a catch..."

"What?"

"You have to share them with your husband..."

"I know that – I thought you were gonna say something else..." she laughed...

"Hmmm... Troy?"

"Yea Bazil?"

"Is there something you'd like your wife to do for you?" he asked mischievously...

"Oh that's that bullshit!" Keisha snapped...

"Hole up – I like this..."

"Troy!"

"What?" he answered as he went over to Keisha, pulled her close to him, and kissed her...

"Nothin'... never mind..." she sighed...

"That's what I thought..." Troy said as he started tickling her...

"Troy..." she laughed... "Stop..."

"Say please..."

"Please..." she said as she put her arms around his neck... "Don't..." she said as she kissed him again... "Ever... Stop..."

"That's what I'm talkin' about..."

"You should get married with us..." I said...

"We're already married..." Keisha laughed...

"We're gonna renew our vows in the court house..."

"That ain't romantic!" Keisha snapped...

"It is for me..." I sighed...

"Why?"

"Because... that's where I got my life back..." I sighed...

"I'on know... I don't wanna get married in a court room..." Keisha sighed...

"Oooohhh..." I sighed...

"What Beautiee?" Bazil asked...

"We can get married on the beach... by the water..." I sighed...

"I like that..." Keisha said...

"Then we can go to the Stonebridge Restaurant..." I sighed...

"Now that's romantic..." Keisha said...

"When y'all wanna do this?" Troy asked...

"Valentine's Day..." I sighed...

"Valentine's Day?" Bazil asked...

"Valentine's Day..." Keisha and I both answered in unison...

"Damn – that's not enough time – we need to hire a wedding planner, a photographer..."

"Troy?" I interrupted...

"Yea..."

"All we need is Judge Duffey, a photographer... and... each other..." I said as I pulled Bazil into a kiss...

"Okay – we need to make reservations – you, Bazil, me, Troy..." Keisha started to say...

"Joselyn, Sam, Sheila, her husband, Smalls, Josefina..."

"Okay – I'm on it..." Keisha said as she picked up her cell phone and called the restaurant...

"Thank you for calling Stonebridge Restaurant – may I make a reservation for you?"

"Yes Maam – we need a table for 12 people on Valentine's Day..."

"Okay – good thing you called – we're already getting filled up... hang on... okay – we have a table at 7pm – how's that?"

"That's fine..."

"Great – let's get you booked before it's gone – may I have your name?"

"Bazil Osgood..."

"Mrs. Osgood – congratulations – are you celebrating Valentine's Day?"

"This is her friend Keisha – but thank you..." Keisha laughed..."

"Oh – I'm sorry – you're welcome..." the hostess laughed...

"We're all renewing our vows..."

"Oh how nice! Okay – we require a deposit for large parties..."

"Bazil – they need your credit card..." Keisha said as she snapped her finger at Bazil...

"Here..." Bazil laughed as he handed his card to her...

"Okay – I got it – y'all take American Express?"

"Yes Maam – I'm ready..."

"Okay – the number is 543-60-1432..."

"Expiration?"

"10/22..."

"Okay – You're all set – please let Mr. Osgood know there's a $500 hold on his card to

145

guarantee the reservation – the $500 deposit will be applied to the bill – there's no refunds – but I'm sure we won't have to worry about that..." she laughed...

"Sure won't!" Keisha laughed...

"Okay – thank you – have a great day!"

"You too..."

"What'd she say?" Bazil asked...

"They put a $500 hold on your card – the $500 will be applied to the bill – the reservation is at 7pm..."

"I'm so excited!" I squealed as I hugged Keisha...

"Me too!"

"I guess I better let Smalls know so he can get in touch with Judge Duffey..." Bazil said as he picked up his cell phone...

"Hello Bazil..."

"Hello Smalls..."

"We're renewing our vows on Valentine's Day..."

"That's what's up!"

"We'd like you and Josefina to join us..."

"We'll be there..."

"You don't understand..."

"What?"

"We want you to renew your vows too..."

"Aww man..." Smalls said... and then it got quiet...

"Smalls? You there?"

"Yea man... I'm here..."

"You alright?"

"I fuckin' love y'all!"

"We love you too…"

"So where we doin' this?"

"Milford Beach…"

"Oh wow…"

"Then we're all going to dinner at the Stonebridge Restaurant…"

"All?"

"Me, Beautiee, you, Josefina, Troy, Keisha, Sam, Joselyn, Sheila, Henley, Judge Duffey, his wife…"

"Wait – you want Judge Duffey to perform the ceremony? Oh wow! So… y'all good?"

"We're good…"

"You're a better man than me…"

"No I'm not…"

"So… you're okay with him performing the ceremony?"

"Smalls?"

"Yea?"

"My wife wants to get married…"

"I know…"

"She's happy…"

"Understood – I'll speak to my wife – and I'll contact Judge Duffey…" he said as he hung up… "We're all set…" Bazil said as he hung up…

"What if Judge Duffey can't do it?" Keisha asked…

"There's too many Justice of the Peace in Connecticut – somebody will marry us on Valetine's Day!" I laughed…

"You right!" Keisha laughed…

"C'mon Keisha –let's go home..." Troy said as he pulled Keisha into a hug...

"Alright y'all – we'll see you later..." Keisha said as they walked out arm in arm...

"Mrs. Osgood?"

"Yes Mr. Osgood?"

"Come with me..." he said as he picked up the envelope, took me by the hand, and led me upstairs to the bedroom. I watched Bazil put the dvd in the player and I started crying when our wedding started playing... "Dance with me..." Bazil said as he pulled me into his arms and we started dancing...

"I love you..."

"I love you too..."

"I'm surprised they didn't see this..."

"I didn't want them to..." he breathed as he held me tighter. We continued dancing until the song was over and then we sat on the bed and continued watching... "Beautiee..." Bazil whispered as he started crying...

"My Thirst Quencher..." I whispered as I started crying too. We watched the wedding until it was finished, Bazil laid me back on the bed, and we started kissing feverishly...

"Do you remember our wedding night?" Bazil breathed...

"Yeesss..." I breathed...

"Are you thirsty?"

"Thirsty... and hungry..."

"Oh... that's right... we didn't eat..."

"I need you to feed me..."

"Is that right?"

"Yeesss...."

"Mmmm.... Which appetite would you like me to satisfy first?"

"All of them..."

"Okay – I'll be right back!" he said as he jumped up out of bed and ran downstairs...

"I should'a told him to fuck me first..." I sighed as I sat back on the bed and waited for Bazil to come back upstairs. Bazil came into the bedroom with the unfinished bottle of champagne and two glasses...

"I'll be right back!" he said as he ran out the room and downstairs again. When he came back he had the sandwiches Keisha made on two plates on a tray...

'I was starting to think I should 'a told you to fuck me first..." I laughed...

"I can do that..." he said as he put the try on the dresser...

"Oh no – that's okay – I want it now!" I laughed...

"Is that right?" Bazil asked as he smiled at me mischievously...

"Yes..."

"As you wish..." he said as he came over to the bed, pulled me down on my back, spread my legs, and ease himself inside me...

"Bazil..."

"Is this what you want?"

"Yesss...."

"Ummph...   Ummph...   Ummph... Ummph..." Bazil put his arms under my back, held me, kissed me, and stroked me deeper...

"Hmmph...   Hmmph...   Hmmph... Hmmph..."

"Ummph...   Ummph...   Ummph... Ummph..."

"Hmmph...   Hmmph...   Hmmph... Hmmph..."

"Ummph...   Ummph...   Ummph... Ummph..."

"Hmmph...   Hmmph...   Hmmph... Hmmph..."

"UMMPH...   UMMPH...   UMMPH... UMMPH..."

"HMMPH...   HMMPH...   HMMPH... HMMPH..."

"Ummph..."

"Hmmph..."

"Ummph..."

"Hmmph"

"I love you Mrs. Osgood..."

"I love you Mr. Osgood...

"I remember when you started working with me..."

"Mmmm Hmmm..."

"You came into the office..."

"Mmmm Hmmm..."

"You locked the door..."

"Mmmm Hmmm..."

"You said you had this fantasy..."

"Mmmm Hmmm..."

"Of being fucked by your boss...

"Mmmm Hmmm..."

"On his desk..."

"Mmmm Hmmm..."

"You couldn't be quiet..." he laughed...

"Mmmm Hmmm..."

"One day..."

"Mmmm Hmmm..."

"I wanna try something..."

"Mmmm Hmmm..."

"I want us to fuck..."

"Mmmm Hmmm..."

"And see who can go the longest..."

"Mmmm Hmmm..."

"Without making noise..."

"Mmmm Hmmm..."

"But today..."

"Mmmm Hmmm..."

"Is not that day..."

"Mmmm Hmmm..."

"So... we're gonna eat..."

"Mmmm Hmmm..."

"We're gonna drink..."

"Mmmm Hmmm..."

"And then... we're gonna make a lotta noise..." he laughed as we continued kissing.

Chapter 14

"Welcome back!" Sam said as we walked into the office... 'How are you feeling?"

"Where's Joselyn?" I asked...

"She's in her office – you need me to get her?"

"Yes – and Sheila too..."

"Yes Maam..." Sam said as he turned to leave...

"Sam?"

"Yes Maam?"

"Mrs. Osgood..."

"Oh – sorry... Mrs. Osgood – I'll be right back..." he said as he went to get Sheila and Joselyn..."

"Good morning – welcome back..." Sheila said as she came into our office smiling...

"Good morning – thank you – Joselyn?"

"Yes Mrs. Osgood?"

"Are you okay?"

"Yea... I'm okay..."

"I asked Sam to get you because I have an important announcement..."

"Okay – who's getting fired?" Sheila laughed...

"I don't know yet – but that's not why I wanted to see you..." I said as Bazil put his arm around me and pulled me close to him...

"We're getting married again..." Bazil said...

"Congratulations!" Sam said as he pulled us into a hug...

"We'd like you to join us..."

"Huh?" Sheila asked...

"We're renewing our vows on Valentine's Day – on the beach – and we'd like you to celebrate with us and renew your vows too..." I said...

"Sam and Joselyn can do that – you don't need me and Henley..." Sheila laughed...

"Sheila... my wife would like you and Henley to join us..." Bazil said...

"I'll talk to Henley tonight..."

"Thank you Sheila..." I sighed as I pulled her into a hug...

"We'll be there..." Sam said...

"Thank you Sam..." I sighed as I pulled him into a hug...

"So what do you need me to do?" Joselyn sighed...

"Joselyn?"

"Yes Mrs. Osgood?"

"The only thing I need you to do is show up on the beach, renew your vows with Sam, and join us at the Stonebridge Restaurant for dinner..."

"What time?" she sighed...

"Wedding at 5pm – dinner at 7pm..."

"Do we have to come back to work the next day?"

"Joselyn – Valentine's Day is on Friday – you don't work on Saturdays..." I laughed...

"Sam – I need to go over a few things with you..." Bazil said...

"Okay – we can do that now if you want..." Sam said as they walked out of the office...

"I need to go finish my quarterly reports..." Sheila said...

"Okay – I'll see you later..." I said as Sheila left...

"I need to go now..." Joselyn said as she got up to leave...

"Joselyn?"

"Yes Mrs. Osgood?"

"Close the door..."

"Okay..." she sighed as she closed the door...

"Who's the Bitch?"

"Excuse me?"

"If somebody's fuckin' with you – tell me who she is so I can take her out – you know I will!"

"Mrs. Osgood..." Joselyn laughed... "I can't..."

"That's better!" I snapped...

"What?"

"You're laughing..."

"Yea..."

"So... are you gonna tell me who's making you feel the way you're feeling?"

"I can't say..."

"Why? Is it your mother?"

"Mrs. Osgood... it's not my mother..."

"Well – who is it then?"

"It's you..."

"Me?"

"Yea..."

"Umm... I just got outta jail..."

"I know – see – I shouldn't a told you..."

"Joselyn – I don't understand..."

"Mrs. Osgood – you promoted me – and I'm grateful... but..."

"You're tired..."

"Yea... I'm sorry..."

"You don't need to apologize..."

"Yes I do..."

"No – you don't – before I got here, MaryJane LaRue was passing you most of her work – now that she's not here – you're doing all her work..."

"Yea..."

"I'm going to change that effective immediately..." I said as I got up..."

"So does that mean I'm being demoted?"

"Not at all – come with me..." I said as Joselyn got up to follow me..."

"Where are we going?"

"To the cafeteria – I need you to make us both a cup of coffee..." I said as we left the office and headed to the cafeteria...

"Hey Joselyn..." Cheryl said as we walked into the cafeteria...

"Hey Cheryl..." Joselyn replied...

"Welcome back Mrs. Osgood..."

"Thank you Cheryl – I need to speak with you – I'll be down to see you after we have coffee..."

"Is everything okay?"

"Everything's fine – I'll see you in a few..." I said as I sat down at the table...

"Here's your coffee Mrs. Osgood..." Joselyn said as she put our coffee on the table and sat down...

"Okay Joselyn – I need to get you up to speed...

"Okay..." she sighed...

"I'm going to tell my story..."

"Okay..."

"Joselyn – you don't understand..."

"I don't..." she laughed...

"Here..." I said as I pulled out my pad and she started reading...

"Oh wow..."

"Yea..."

"So... you're going to publish your story?"

"Yea..."

"Are you going to tell everything?"

"I might..."

"Oh – so I'm gonna have more responsibility..." she laughed...

"Not necessarily..."

"Okay – wait – I don't get it..."

"Have you ever been a supervisor?"

"I was a supervisor at my other job..."

"Okay good – I'm going to hire an intern – she'll report to you – you can give her work as you see fit – this will free you up for my personal project..."

"Mrs. Osgood?"

"Yes Joselyn?"

"You were planning to do this before you came in today – weren't you?"

"Yes..."

"Okay..."

"So... how's it sound?"

"Well... I appreciate it... but..."

"What?"

"I don't want to take the time to train somebody and then they don't work out..."

"Joselyn – you used to work for your husband – right?"

"Yes..."

"So – your husband has been without an assistant for a while – you train the intern – if she works out – she works for Sam – and you work for us exclusively..."

"Hmmm... okay..."

"I'm going to contact the Fairfield County Business Council and ask them to send us a few people to interview..."

"You're not going to post the job?"

"No – the Business Council has a program – 40 Stars Under 40 – they're already screened – it'll save us a lot of time – and you won't have to worry about them not working out..."

"What if they don't like the publishing business?"

"The Business Council will only send people that are interested in publishing, so that won't be an issue..."

"Okay... I guess I'm a supervisor now..."

"Yes you are – you go tell Sam – I'll go see Cheryl..."

"Hey!" Sam said as Joselyn walked into his office..."

"Hey..." Joselyn sighed...

"You need a minute?" Bazil asked...

"Yea..." Joselyn sighed...

"Okay – I'll go back to my office – Sam – we can finish up later..." Bazil said as he left. Sam got up to close the door and then he went to pull Joselyn into a hug...

"Babe... what's wrong?"

"I don't know where to start..."

"We can start here..." he said as he kissed her..."

"That's nice..." Joselyn breathed as she kissed him back...

"Okay... now tell me..."

"I got another promotion..."

"Whaatt???"

"I'm a supervisor now..."

"Okay – why aren't you happy?"

"I'm happy... but..."

"Joselyn... come sit down..." Sam said as he led her to the loveseat and she sat down beside him... "What's wrong?"

"Mrs. Osgood is publishing her story..."

"Ooohhh..."

"She said she's hiring an intern..."

"Okay..."

"I'm going to train the intern..."

"Okay..."

"And if she works out... she'll work with you... and I'll be working for them exclusively..."

"Oh... I get it..."

"You do?"

"You wanna work with me... and you want the intern to work with them..."

"Yes!" Joselyn breathed...

"Joselyn?"

"Yes Sam?"

"This is a good thing..."

"It is?"

"Absolutely..."

"How?"

"You're getting another promotion..."

"I know..."

"That's more money..."

"I know... but..."

"How long did you work here before you got promoted – the 1st time?"

"A long time..."

"You used to complain to your mother all the time about having to do MaryJane's work... and you never got compensated for it..."

"True..."

"Mr. Osgood gets married – as soon as his wife comes in here – you get promoted..."

"The only reason I got promoted is because MaryJane got fired…"

"That's not true… and you know it…"

"Sam!"

"Mrs. Osgood could have hired an intern to replace MaryJane instead of promoting you – but she saw something in you right away…"

"All I did was be nice to her…"

"Joselyn… you've been working so hard… you don't see what's happening in front of you…"

"I don't get it…"

"Joselyn – Mrs. Osgood sees what we all see in you – yes – you were nice to her – but Mrs. Osgood saw beyond that – she offered you a promotion – you accepted it – you've been working so hard – I know you're tired – she knows you're tired – and she offered you another promotion – she's hiring an intern – she loves you…"

"Yea… she loves me alright – she wants me to work on her project…"

"Of course she does – she doesn't trust anybody else – but she trusts you…"

"Yea…" Joselyn sighed as she started smiling…

"So… you know what this means…" Sam said as he started kissing her on her neck…

"What does this mean Sam?"

"You won't have to work so hard…"

"And?" Joselyn laughed as Sam continued kissing her on her neck…

"We'll have more time…"

"This is true..." Joselyn laughed...

"So..."

"We can start working on having a baby..." Joselyn sighed as she turned to Sam, put her arms around his neck, and pulled him into a kiss...

"Girl! Where you get that shit from?"

"My Aunt Gert works at the jail..."

"What?!"

"Yea girl! She told me Beautiee got it in from the first night she was in there!"

"Damn – I didn't know she got down like that – I'm glad she ain't made at me..." Tracy laughed...

"You – shit – I'm lucky I still have a job after I told you I'da beat her ass!"

"Girl – you ain't neva lie – but from what I just saw, I hope MaryJane stayed away from her husband – Beautiee's no joke..."

"I'm so glad my Aunt sent me this video!"

"Me too girl – I can't believe it – Beautiee's gangster!"

"Yes I am..." I said as I walked into payroll, interrupting their conversation...

"Mrs. Osgood – oh my God – I'm..."

"Tracy – go back to your desk – Cheryl – I need to speak with you..."

"Yyyesss... Mrs. Osgood?"

"We're going to be hiring an intern – I need you to get started on the paperwork..."

"What will her salary be?"

"Her starting salary will be $35k – we'll cap it at $40k..."

"Okay – I'll get right on it..."

"Thank you – oh – Cheryl?"

"Yes Mrs. Osgood?"

"When you're done – I need to see you in my office..." I said as I made a beeline to Sheila's office...

"Hello Mrs. Osgood..."

"Hello Sheila – I need to see you and Tracy in my office..." I said as I walked out before she could ask me any questions...

"Hi Mrs. Osgood – I..."

"Joselyn – I need to see you and Sam in my office..." I said as I walked away before she could ask me any questions..."

"Beautiee..." Bazil breathed as he pulled me into a kiss...

"Thank you..." I breathed... "I needed that..."

"You're welcome..." he said as he kissed me again... "Now what's wrong?"

"Mrs. Osgood?"

"Yes Joselyn?"

"We're here..."

"Come in..." I said as Joselyn, Sam, Sheila, Tracy, and Cheryl came into the office...

"Thank you for coming..." I said as I went to close the door... "First – effective immediately – Joselyn is now supervising Tracy as well as the new intern we're hiring..."

"I am?" Joselyn asked...

162

"You are..."

"Umm... Thank you!"

"You're welcome – Joselyn – Cheryl – make Joselyn's raise effective today..."

"Yes Mrs. Osgood..."

"Second – Tracy – Joselyn will be supervising you as well as training you to take over some of her duties..."

"Why I gotta take on more work?" I barely have enough time to do the work Mrs. Henley gives me to do!"

"Well Tracy – you might get more work done if you spent more time at your desk – and less time in payroll gossiping with Cheryl..." Sheila looked over at Tracy, looked over at Cheryl, and looked back at me...

"Third – the new intern we hire will be Sam's new personal assistant – Joselyn will be working for me and my husband exclusively...

"Is there anything else you need?" Cheryl asked...

"Yes – Sam, Joselyn, Sheila, Tracy – you're excused – Joselyn – I need you to set up a meeting with Tracy so you can start training her – she needs to be brought up to speed as soon as possible so you'll be able to focus on training the new intern..."

"Yes Mrs. Osgood – Tracy – I'll meet with you after lunch..." Joselyn smiled as she walked out the office with Sam. Sheila and Tracy left after Joselyn and Cheryl turned to leave...

"Cheryl? Close the door..."

"Yes Mrs. Osgood?"

"You should be fired..."

"Why? What'd I do?" the gasped...

"Beautiee? What's going on?" Bazil asked...

"I had a meeting with Joselyn earlier – we were discussing hiring an intern – I told her I was going to see Cheryl..."

"Okay..."

"When I got to payroll, Cheryl was gossiping with Tracy..."

"Mrs. Osgood – please – I can explain..."

"Cheryl – let my wife finish..." Bazil said...

"They were gossiping about me..."

"Mrs. Osgood... please..."

"Cheryl! Let my wife finish!" Bazil boomed...

"Yes Mr. Osgood..." she sighed as she sat down...

"Apparently, Cheryl's Aunt Gertrude works at the prison..."

"Is that right?" Bazil asked as his eyes turned to slits...

"Yes Mr. Osgood..." Cheryl sighed...

"So... remember the night I was in a fight?"

"Beautiee... what's this got to do with Cheryl?" Bazil asked...

"Chery's Aunt recorded the fight – and she sent the video to Cheryl..."

"WHAT?! Is this true Cheryl?!" Bazil yelled...

"Yess..." Cheryl sighed...

"Cheryl and Tracy we're watching the video when I interrupted them..." I explained...

"That's it – I've heard enough – you're fired – get the hell outta my office!" Bazil yelled...

"Noo... please... I'm sorry!" Cheryl cried...

"Bazil... wait..." I said as I stood there thinking...

"Yes Beautiee?"

"Let's not fire Cheryl..."

"Beautiee... are you sure?"

"Cheryl – you can keep your job... if you do two things for us..." I said...

"What do you need me to do?" she sniffed...

"I need you to give my husband the video..."

"Mrs. Osgood – I can't – my Aunt could lose her job..."

"And you could lose yours..."

"Fine..." she sighed as she took out her phone and handed it to Bazil... "What else do you need me to do?"

"I need you to keep this between us..."

"I don't understand..."

"I need you to keep this between us – that means no more gossiping – no more sharing – and this is most important – DON'T MENTION THIS TO YOUR AUNT – AM I CLEAR?"

"Yes Mrs. Osgood..." she sighed...

"Cheryl?"

"Yes Mr. Osgood?"

"Does anybody else have a copy of the video?"

"Tracy..." Bazil picked up the phone and called Sheila...

"I need to see Tracy in my office..." he said and then he hung up...

"You wanted to see me?" Tracy asked as she came into the office...

"Give me your phone..." Bazil demanded...

"Excuse me?"

"I SAID GIVE ME YOUR PHONE!" Bazil boomed...

"Hhhheeerrreee..." Tracy stuttered as she took her phone out her purse and gave it to him...

"Hmmmm... Ahhh... there it is!" Bazil said as he deleted the video and handed her phone back to her...

"Wait... oh – see this some bullshit!" Tracy snapped...

"Tracy!" Cheryl exclaimed...

"No Cheryl – fuck that – first I gotta take on more work – now they deletin' shit off my phone – fuck this – I quit!" she said as she stormed out the office. Bazil picked up the phone and called Sam...

"Sam – Tracy just quit... yes... that's right... I need you to make sure her access is blocked – and she's to be escorted off the premises... thank you Sam..." he said as he hung up... "Cheryl?"

"Yes Mr. Osgood?"

"Please process paperwork for two interns..."

"Yes Mr. Osgood – thank you for giving me another chance..."

"Thank my wife..."

"Thank you Mrs. Osgood!" Cheryl squealed as she ran out the office... and Sheila ran in...

"What happened? Did Tracy get fired?"

"Tracy quit..." Bazil answered...

"Doesn't matter to me – now maybe I can get somebody that'll actually do some work..."

"You've been having a problem with Tracy? Why didn't you say anything?"

"Well... you had enough going on with your wife – I didn't want to bother you..."

"Sheila?"

"Yes Mr. Osgood?"

"Don't ever feel you can't talk to me if you're having an issue with an employee..."

"Okay – now that you've said that – I need a replacement..." Sheila laughed...

"Cheryl is processing paperwork for two interns – we'll start interviewing right away..."

"Thank you Mr. Osgood..."

"What happened?" Joselyn asked as she came running into the office...

"Tracy quit!" Sheila squealed...

"What? Why?"

"She actually said this some bullshit – fuck this..." Bazil answered...

"WWHHHAAATTT?!"

"I guess she really didn't want to do anymore work..." Sheila laughed...

"Joselyn – please call the Business Council for me – we need to set up interviews asap – and I need you and Sheila to sit in on the interviews..."

"What about Sam?" Joselyn asked...

"Yes – Sam too..."

"Yes Mrs. Osgood – Sam..." she called on her way out...

"Do you need me for anything?" Sheila asked...

"No Sheila – thank you." I waited for Sheila to leave and then I got up and locked the door...

"C'mere..." Bazil said as he pulled me into a hug...

"When will it fuckin' end?" I sighed...

"I'm calling Smalls..." Bazil said as he picked up the phone...

"Hello Bazil..." Smalls said as Bazil put the phone on speaker...

"Hello..."

"I'm glad you called – I have news..."

"I hope it's good news..." I sighed...

"Judge Duffey said yes..."

"Aww... that makes me happy..." I sighed...

"What's wrong?" Smalls asked...

"I'm sending you a video..." Bazil answered...

"A video? What now?"

"One of my employees had a video in her phone..."

"Oh God – Bazil – what'd you do?"

"I'm sending it now..." Bazil said as he sent the video...

"Hole up... what the fuck?"

"Exactly..." Bazil sighed...

"Beautiee... I'm sorry..."

"So am I..." I sighed...

"Wait – you said one of your employees had this video?"

"Actually – it was two of them..." Bazil sighed...

"What the fuck – how – where – I can't!"

"There's a guard at the prison named Gertrude..." I explained...

"Oh shit – she recorded you?"

"Yes..."

"And she sent it to one of your employees?!" Smalls yelled...

"Her niece is our payroll supervisor..." Bazil sighed...

"Yo – you fire that Bitch?"

"Beautiee won't let me..."

"Beautiee! Why?"

"Because... you keep your friends close... and your enemies' closer..."

"Beautiee?'

'Yes Smalls?"

"Never mind – did she send it to anybody else?"

"She did..."

"Dammit! Fire her ass!"

"I deleted the video from the other employee's phone – and she quit..." Bazil explained...

"How you know she didn't send it to anyone else?"

"She has a company phone – we monitor all downloads, sites they visit, texts, and tweets..."

"Damn – she's stupid!"

"She was..."

"So why won't you fire the other lady?"

"Smalls?"

"Yes Beautiee?"

"I have her in the palm of my hand – and when I need her to... she'll do my bidding..."

"How can you be sure?"

"Because she needs her job..."

"I still think you should fire her ass!"

"In time Smalls... in time..."

"I'ma hold onto this... for now..."

"Thank you Smalls...' Bazil said as he hung up.... "Mrs. Osgood – I need you to come with me..." Bazil said as he took me by the hand and led me out the office... "Sam?"

"Yes Mr. Osgood..."

"We'll be out of the office for a few hours..."

"Okay – see you later..." Sam said as Bazil led me down the corridor, out the building, and into the parking lot.

Chapter 15

"Where would you like to go?" Bazil asked...

"Fridays..."

"Fridays it is..." he said as he drove out the parking lot. We didn't say anything on the way. Bazil picked up my hand, kissed it, and we rode the rest of the way in silence. After we got to Fridays, Bazil drove around for a few minutes looking for a parking space... "I didn't think it would be so crowded at this time of day..."

"I guess I'm not the only one that needs a drink..." I sighed. Bazil parked the car and we went inside...

"Welcome to Fridays – table for two?"

"Table for two..." Bazil acknowledged...

"Follow me..." the hostess said as we followed her to our table and sat down... "Your waitress will be right with you..." the hostess said as she gave us menus and walked away...

"Beautiee... I'm sorry..."

"I'm thirsty..." I said as I smiled at him mischievously...

"Welcome to Fridays – my name is Lashonda – may I start you off with something to drink?"

"I'd like a pomegranate margarita..." I said...

"And for you sir?"

"I'd like some Hennessey…"

"Straight up or on the rocks?"

"On the rocks…"

"Okay – I'll be back with your drinks…" she said as she left…

"Beautiee…" Bazil said as he took my hands… "Are you okay?"

"Yea…" I sighed…

"Here's your drinks…" the waitress said as she placed them on the table… "Are you ready to order?"

"I'll have the bucket of bones…" I said…

"Make that two…" Bazil said…

"Okay – I'll be back…" the waitress said as she went to place our order…

"Beautiee?"

"Yes Bazil?"

"Talk to me…"

"Okay…" I said and then I gulped my drink down…

"Beautiee…"

"I was nervous about going back to work…"

"I know…"

"Before I went to the cafeteria I asked Joselyn who the Bitch was…"

"What?"

"I told her to tell me who was fuckin' with her so I could take 'em out – and she laughed…"

"I love you…" Bazil laughed as he leaned across the table and kissed me…"

"I asked her to tell me who was responsible for making her feel the way she was feeling..."

"Did you find out who it was?"

"She said it was me..."

"What?"

"Yea..."

"I'm surprised... and disappointed..."

"Don't be..."

"Why?"

"Joselyn's been working really hard since I promoted her..."

"True..."

"She's been doing two jobs for a long time..."

"That's true too..."

"She's tired..."

"I didn't realize that..."

"I know..."

"So that's why you decided to hire the intern?"

"Actually... no..."

"Here's your bucket of bones..." the waitress said as she placed our food in front of us... "May I get you another drink?"

"Yes please..." I said as we started eating...

"Water for me..." Bazil said..."

"I planned on hiring an intern because I need Joselyn for my project..."

"Oh so you were planning on hiring an intern anyway..."

"Yea..."

"And then you went to payroll..."

"Nobody was supposed to see that..." I whispered as I teared up. Bazil got up from his seat, came over to where I was sitting, and held me... "You didn't even see that – and those two Bitches were watching it – and laughing..." I said as I started crying...

"I know..." Bazil said as he pulled me into a kiss...

"What if I didn't walk in on them? They probably would've passed that video all over – and everyone would be laughing at us! What if she put the video online?"

"Beautiee – she didn't..."

"How do you know?" I sniffed...

"Because... just like Cheryl needs her job... Gertrude needs her job too..."

"Why'd she have to record me?"

"Because you're my wife..." Bazil sighed...

"Here's your drink..." the waitress said as she placed my drink on the table... "Can I get you anything else?"

"Yes – water please..."

"Okay..." she said as she went to get me water...

"You should let me fire Cheryl..."

"No..."

"Why not?"

"The City of Bridgeport owes you... now they're gonna owe me... and I intend to collect..."

"Beautiee... what are you going to do?"

"I'm gonna drink..." I said as I picked up my drink and gulped it down...

"I'm gonna eat..." I said as I picked up some ribs... "And... when the time is right... I'm gonna be just what Tracy said I am..." I said as I finished my ribs...

"What's that?"

"Gangster..." I answered as I pulled Bazil into a kiss and kissed him hard...

"Are you ready to go back to the office?"

"I'm not sure – what will it be this time?" I sighed as we got up from the table, left the money to pay the check, and headed back to the office.

Chapter 16

"Mrs. Osgood, I have Marsha Gordon on the phone…" Joselyn said as we walked in…

"Oh – that's great – transfer her to my line…" I said as I hurried into my office…

"Hi Marsha…" I breathed…

"Hello Beautiee – did I catch you at a bad time?"

"Not at all – I'm just getting back from lunch…"

"Oh that's great – I wanted to talk to you about the interns you wanted from us…"

"Okay…"

"First – I want to thank you for choosing the Business Council for your needs…"

"You're welcome…"

"We're very happy to work with your publishing company and we believe this will be an exciting opportunity for the people we've chosen…"

"I agree – I asked Joselyn to call you rather than post an ad because I knew you were going to send us qualified interns…"

"Oh that's nice – thank you for saying that…"

"You're welcome…"

"Okay – we have two interns we feel would be an excellent fit for your publishing company…"

"Okay…"

"Our first choice is A'Licia Henley – she has a Bachelor's Degree in Finance Administration. She earned her Bachelor's Degree while she was working for Stamford Hospital…"

"Hmmm… okay…"

"Our second choice is Shadajah Logan. Shadajah just earned her Bachelor's Degree in Communications. She's young – she doesn't have any experience, but we think she'll really excel with your company…"

"Okay…"

"So… what do you think?"

"Send them both…"

"Really? That's great!"

"They have to be interviewed…"

"Of course…"

"I'll let you in on something…"

"Okay…"

"When I asked Joselyn to call you, we only needed one intern – after Joselyn called you, another position became available – so now we need two interns…"

"Are you telling me you're going to hire both of them?"

"As long as they interview well…"

"Oh that's great – so will you be interviewing them?"

"It will be me, my husband, the Vice CEO, the CFO, and our Personal Assistant, Joselyn…"

"Oh wow – a panel interview – A'Licia will handle that with no problem – I'm not sure how Shadajah will react though..."

"She had a degree in communications – she'll do fine..."

"I'm sure you're right – when can I send them over?"

"How about tomorrow morning at 10?"

"Okay – they'll be there..."

"Thank you Marsha..."

"You're welcome..." she said as she hung up...

"How's Marsha?" Bazil asked...

"She's really happy – she's sending us two interns – I told her if they interview well we'll probably hire both of them..."

"I'm sure she was glad to hear that..."

"She was..."

"So what time will they be here?"

"Tomorrow morning at 10..."

"That's good..." Bazil said as he got up and locked the door...

"Mr. Osgood... what are you up to?" I asked as I smiled at him mischievously...

"You..." he answered as he came over to me, pulled me up out my chair, and kissed me...

"Mmmm... I love when you do that..."

"Is that right?" he asked as he kissed me again...

"Mmmm... Yeesss..." I breathed as Bazil put his tongue in my mouth and we started tonguing each other down...

"Shall we continue this on the desk?" Bazil asked...

"We can't..."

"We can..."

"We'll be interrupted..." and just as I said that, there was a knock on the door...

"Mrs. Osgood?"

"Yes Joselyn?" I sighed...

"Can I come in?"

"Just a sec..." I said as I went to unlock the door...

"Sorry to disturb you..."

"Joselyn – you're not disturbing us..." I laughed...

"Are we getting interns?"

"They'll be here tomorrow morning at 10..."

"They?"

"Yes Joselyn – we'll be interviewing two interns..."

"Oh wow – I like that..."

"So do I..." I said as I got up...

"Beautiee – where do you think you're going? I'm not done with you..." Bazil said...

"Okay – bye!" Joselyn laughed as she left the office and I got up, locked the door, and went back over to Bazil...

"Yes Mr. Osgood?"

"Come here..." he said as he stood up and pulled me into a kiss... "Where were you going?"

"I was going to payroll..." I breathed...

"Why?" he asked before he kissed me again...

"Mmmm... because..."

"Because?" he asked as he kissed me again...

"Bazil... stop..." I laughed...

"Why?"

"Because" I answered as he started kissing me on my neck... "I can't concentrate..."

"Okay..." he laughed... "I'll stop..."

'Marsha is sending us two interns..."

"Yes... I know..."

"One of them has a degree in Finance Administration..."

"Oh wow..."

"She also worked for Stamford Hospital..."

"Okay – c'mon – let's go to payroll..." Bazil said as he took me by the hand and we walked down the hall towards payroll...

"Hi Mr. Osgood – Hi Mrs. Osgood..." some of the employees said as we walked in...

"Good afternoon – is Cheryl here?" I asked...

"I'm here Mrs. Osgood – what can I do for you?"

"Hello Cheryl..." Bazil said...

"Good afternoon..." Cheryl replied nervously...

"Cheryl – we have two interns coming tomorrow at 10 – one of them has a degree in finance – I need you to change the salary from $35k to $45k – cap at $50k..." I said...

"Hmmm... She'll be making as much money as me and she hasn't even started working here yet..."

"Hmmm... Good for her..." Bazil said deliberately...

"Is it alright if I do this later? I haven't been to lunch yet..."

"That's fine..." I said...

"Thank you Mrs. Osgood – I'll see you later..." she said as she ran out..."

"Oh boy – she's upset..." I said...

"She's lucky she's still employed..." Bazil said as we went back to the office.

Chapter 17

"Hey Girl..." Tracy said as Cheryl sat down...

"Mutha Fuckas!" Cheryl yelled...

"Oh my God – what happened?" Did you get fired?"

"I got fired – by Mr. Osgood – but Mrs. Osgood wouldn't let him fire me!"

"That's great!"

"No-the-hell it isn't..."

"Hi – I'm Lashonda – can I start you out with something to drink?"

"Hell yea – long island ice tea – and I wanna taste the liquor!" Cheryl snapped as she slammed her hand on the table...

"Damn Cheryl – is it that bad?"

"Girl – get you a long island ice tea too – you gotta hear this one..."

"I'll have one too..." Tracy said...

"Okay – I'll be right back with your drinks..." the waitress said as she walked away...

"Girl – why'd you quit?" Cheryl asked...

"I was sick of them!"

"Who?"

"Sheila, Joselyn, Beautiee, and Bazil!"

"Why?"

"Oh please – Sheila's a work-a-holic – Joselyn thinks she God's gift to the world – and

Beautiee has Bazil wrapped around her pussy – poor lil' puppy!"

"Damn!"

"I know I shouldn't've had that video – so what – but I really quit because they gave Joselyn another promotion and then they thought I was gonna take on more work for the same pay…"

"I think you should've stayed there until you found another job – now you can't even get unemployment…"

"Fuck them – workin' for them ain't all it's cracked up to be…"

"I know that's right…" Cheryl said as the waitress placed the drinks on the table…

"Do you know what you'd like to eat?" the waitress asked…

"I'll have a cheeseburger and fries…" Tracy said…

"Me too…' Cheryl said…

"Okay – I'll be back…" the waitress said as she left the table…

"Girl – what happened?" Tracy asked…

"Well – you already know Beautiee heard us talking…"

"Bitch always spying and eavesdropping!"

"So – they called me into the office and told me they needed me to process paperwork for the new intern – so I thought I was good – but Beautiee asked me to stay after Sheila and them left their office…"

"Aww shit!"

"So Beautiee tells Bazil everything she heard and Bazil told me I was fired and he also told me to get the hell out of his office..."

"Oh shit!"

"Girl – I begged them not to fire me – and Beautiee told Bazil to let me keep my job..."

"Well damn! She didn't fight for my ass! Bitch!"

"Girl – Beautiee didn't do that for me – she did it for herself..."

"See? Fuckin' Bitch!"

"Girl – I fucked up..."

"No you didn't..."

"Yes I did – I never should've sent you that video..."

"You're not the one that took the damn video!"

"I still fucked up..."

"How?"

"Beautiee told me I can keep my job under two conditions..."

"Oh shit – what?"

"I had to give them the video..."

"No!"

"I can't say anything to my aunt..." Cheryl sighed...

"Fuck that – I'd tell!"

"I can't!"

"Why not?"

"If I tell – we both lose our jobs – I know I fucked up – but I can't do that to my aunt..."

"She should've thought about that before she took that video..."

"I wish she had..."

"You think they went to the police?"

"No..."

"How you know?"

"My aunt still has her job..."

"I wonder what they're gonna do with the video?"

"They're gonna fuck with me..." Cheryl said as the waitress put the food on the table... "Could you bring us the check?"

"Sure..." the waitress answered as she went to get the check and they started eating...

"Fuck with you how?" Tracy asked...

"Well – I had to do the paperwork for two interns – one has a salary of $35k – cap at $40k..."

"That's what I was making..."

"Yea? Well the other one has a degree in finance –her salary is $45k – cap at $50k!"

"Damn!"

"I said she's making the same money as me and she just started – and Bazil says – hmmm... good for her!"

"Mutha fucka!"

"They got me – and there isn't a fuckin' thing I can do about it..." Cheryl sighed as she finished her food and the waitress brought the check...

"Thanks for lunch..." Tracy said...

"You're welcome – I gotta get back – I'll call you..." Cheryl said as she got up from the table and hurried back...

"Just who I wanted to see..." I said as Cheryl came running in..."

"I'm sorry Mrs. Osgood – I'll get right on that paperwork..." she breathed as she sat at her desk, turned on her computer, and pulled some papers out of her desk...

"How was your liquid lunch?" I whispered...

"Mrs. Osgood – Oh my God – I didn't mean..."

"Cheryl?"

"Yes Mrs. Osgood?"

"Relax..." I said as I left payroll...

"There you are..." Bazil said as I walked back into the office...

"Here I am..." I said as I locked the door and went over to Bazil...

"Did Cheryl finish the paperwork?"

"She's just starting it..." I laughed...

"Really?"

"She had a liquid lunch..."

"Is that right? See – she needs to be..."

"She needs to be left alone..." I said as I pulled him into a kiss...

"Mmmm... if that's what you want..."

"That's what I want... for now..."

"For now?"

"Yes..."

"What are you up to Beautiee?"

"Nothing... yet..."

"Ooohhh... I like the way you think..." he said as he started kissing me on my neck...

"I like the way you feel..." I breathed...

"Mrs. Osgood?"

"Just a sec..." I answered as I went to unlock the door..."

"I have the paperwork you wanted..." Cheryl said as she came into the office...

"Thank you Cheryl – you can go now..." I said...

"Ummm... you don't want to look it over?"

"I'm sure you looked it over before you brought it to me – besides – if there's anything that needs to be corrected, you'll fix it..."

"Yes Mrs. Osgood – will there be anything else?"

"No Cheryl..."

"Okay..." she said as she left and I got up to lock the door again...

"Beautiee..."

"Yes Bazil?"

"Let's go home..."

"Okay..."

"Okay?"

"Yea..."

"You alright?"

"I'm fine..." I sighed...

"No... you're not..."

"I've had enough for today..." I sighed...

"Have you?" Bazil asked as he got up and pulled me into a hug...

"I wasn't talking about you..." I said as I kissed him...

"There you are..." he said as he held the door open, and we walked out arm in arm. When we got home, Bazil couldn't wait... "Come with me..." he said as he walked me backwards towards the library...

"Bazil... no..."

"Did you just tell me no?"

"Yes... I'm sorry..."

"You don't want me?'

"Not in the library... I can't..."

"I'm sorry..." he whispered...

"Let's check the mail..." I said as I snatched the door open and look in the mailbox... "Look – we got a letter from Judge Duffey!" I squealed...

"That's nice..."

"Here – open it!" I squealed again...

"Okay – I'll open it..." he laughed as he opened it and started reading:

Dear Mr. & Mrs. Osgood,

I have to admit it – when I heard from your attorney, I was nervous to say the least; however, once your attorney explained why he was calling, I was pleasantly surprised.

I also have to admit – you are the only couple that has been in my court room for a criminal proceeding and then turn around and ask me to officiate the renewal of your vows, as well as your friends. The fact that you would choose me is, in itself, an honor and a privilege, and I am truly humbled.

I am happy to do this for you. My wife is more excited than I am – especially because she's one of your biggest fans.

I look forward to seeing you and your friends on the beach on Valentine's Day at 5pm.

Cordially,

Judge Duffey

"There you are…" I said as I went up to Bazil, pulled him into a hug, and kissed him…
"Here I am…" he breathed as he kissed me back…
"I'm so happy…"
"So am I…"
"I can't wait until Valentine's Day…"
"Neither can I…"
"Let's go upstairs…"
"Okay" he said as he took my hand and led me upstairs to the bedroom…
"Hello Smalls…" Bazil said as he answered the phone…

"Hello – did you get Judge Duffey's letter?'

"Yeesss…" Bazil breathed as I took his dick out his pants and started stroking it…

"Yo – I'ma call you back…" Smalls laughed as he hung up. Bazil undressed me as I continued playing with his dick and then he pushed me back on the bed, climbed on top of me, eased himself inside me, put his tongue in my mouth, tongued me down, and gave me multiple orgasms for the rest of the afternoon.

<u>Twisted Beautiee Tree</u>

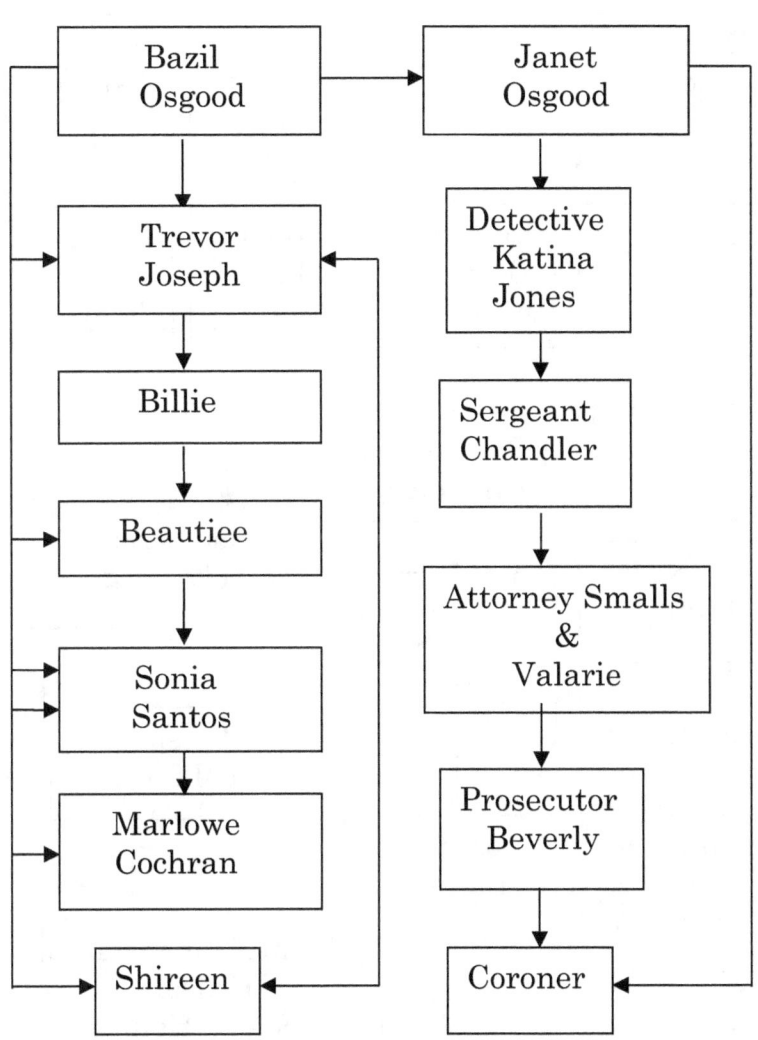

<u>Twisted Beautiee Tree</u>

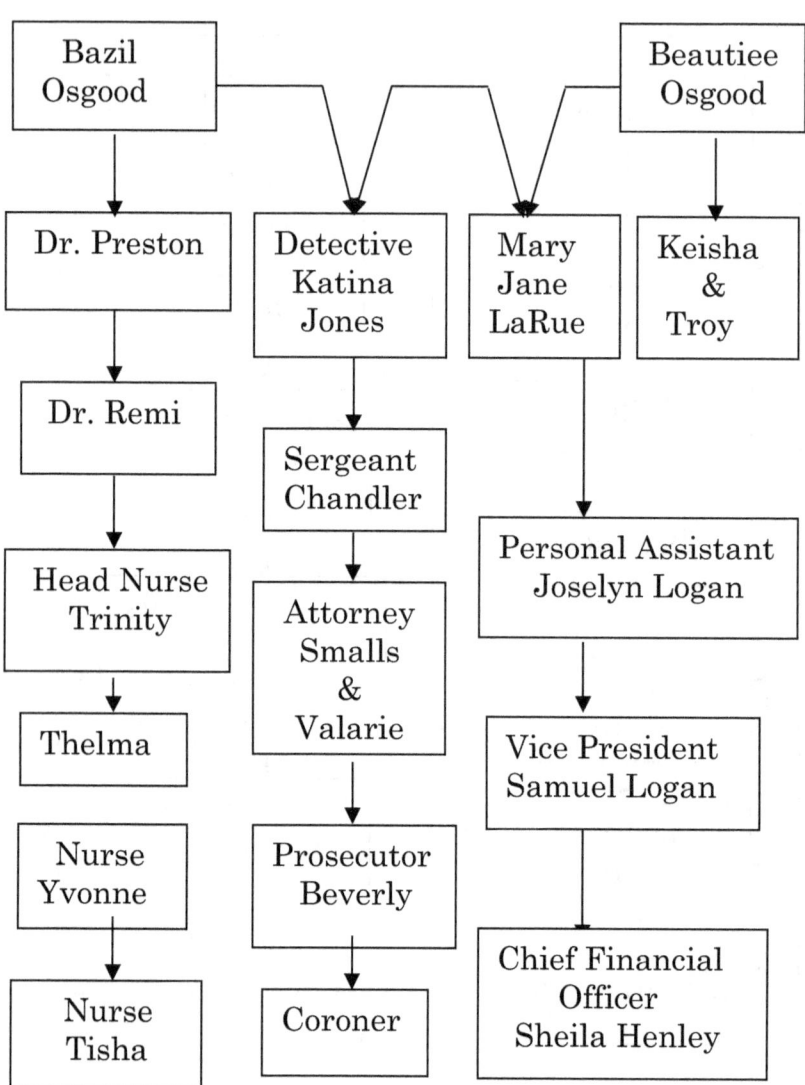

www.ingramcontent.com/pod-product-compliance
Lightning Source LLC
Chambersburg PA
CBHW072110170626
46813CB00004B/1505